MIDNIGHT SOLITAIRE

A novel by
Greg F. Gifune

Published by Crystal Lake Publishing—Tales from The Darkest Depths

Website: www.crystallakepub.com/

WELCOME
TO ANOTHER

CRYSTAL LAKE PUBLISHING
CREATION

Join today at www.crystallakepub.com & www.patreon.com/CLP

For Nikki Grace

"Artists must be sacrificed to their art. Like bees, they must put their lives into the sting they give."

—Ralph Waldo Emerson

ONE

There are no clocks here.

A young woman in a black skirt, white blouse and black pumps sits at a small desk at the very end of a long and narrow hallway. The walls are bare, and the low ceilings and floors match their stark white color. Everything is so clean it has an antiseptic, slightly surreal feel, as if people rarely come here.

The woman, in her early twenties, is tidy, well kempt and has the look of a girl-next-door straight out of Central Casting. Her complexion is flawless, almost eerily so, her hair is pulled back into a bun at the rear of her head, her makeup is applied with precision and restraint, and her fingernails—kept at a modest length—are manicured and painted with a shiny clear gloss.

Her desk, a small, sparse, white unit that fades effortlessly into the background, is completely clear but for a delicate teacup and saucer in its center and a red rotary telephone in the upper right-hand corner that is so bright it looks as if it's been dipped in blood.

She sits quietly in the quiet hallway, back perfectly straight, eyes staring straight ahead at nothing, hands folded neatly in her lap.

After a moment, one of the small lights on the telephone begins to blink. She carefully lifts the receiver, places it to her ear then depresses the button. She listens then replaces the handset without saying a word.

She rises to her feet, and, taking the teacup and saucer with her, slowly makes her way down the long hallway, her heels clacking tile as she goes.

When she reaches the end of the hallway she comes to a closed door. Without hesitation, she presses a series of buttons on a pad to the right of it.

The door opens silently, and she slips through into a small, dimly lit room. A long meeting table faces a large and long panel of glass. Six people sit at the table—five men and one woman—speaking to each other in anxious whispers, nervous with anticipation. Before each of them are open folders or briefcases, and although one of the men, the oldest in the room, is dressed in a military uniform, the others, clad in suits, appear to be civilians. The men and woman are older, sixty or more, but one—a dwarf—is a bit younger, perhaps in his late thirties. Beyond the large glass panel is only darkness, their ghoulish reflections barely discernable in the black glass.

The young woman with the tea moves behind them and carefully places the teacup and saucer down in front of a bloated gray-haired man with bug eyes and pasty, unhealthy-looking skin. Unlike the others, he is not engaged in any sort of conversation, but instead stares at the glass as if attempting to make something happen through sheer will. Next to him is a red rotary phone matching the one on the desk out in the hallway.

He does not seem to notice the woman has put his tea down for him.

She turns and leaves the room without comment.

It is only then that the man raises the teacup to his mouth, delicately, as if afraid he might break it otherwise, and takes a loud, slurping sip. He swallows, puts the cup down and leans forward on the table, resting his flabby chin in his hand and staring intently as ever at the glass.

"Your attention, please," an unnaturally calm, monotone female voice says from a speaker in the ceiling. "It's beginning."

The others cease their conversations and focus on the glass.

Behind it, a light gradually appears and rises, revealing what lies on the other side of the glass.

A room that resembles an operating theater comes into view.

On a table in the center of the room is a nude dark-haired woman lying on her back. She is unconscious and intubated with a breathing tube that runs to a respirator.

And she is more than eight months pregnant.

TWO

The man runs as best he can, hobbling along on one leg as his other drags behind him; useless and flopping about like the snapped and mangled limb it is. He pushes on despite the agonizing pain, moving fast as he can, which is not very fast at all, and shuffles down the middle of the road, using the center lane as a guide in the dark so he doesn't lose his way. Between night and the beginnings of snow flurries swirling about before his eyes, visibility is low. The storm is just beginning, but already skinny serpentine lines of snow slither along the pavement, snakes of salt sidewinding from one lane to the next. His heart pounds his chest and his lungs wheeze and burn in the bitter cold, but he struggles not to cough. Something has broken deep inside him and he knows coughing will only make it worse. He chances a look back over his shoulder into the darkness. No lights. No sign of life or anyone following. Just pitch-black night littered with snow flurries and trails of breath escaping him in smoky spirals. But he knows it's only a matter of time. His pursuer is back there in the dark, toying with him the way a cat allows a mouse to flee to the very edge of its reach before casually snatching it back and snapping its neck.

His dead leg scrapes the ground, the sound mingling with his labored breath and occasional groans of pain. The wind whistles, cutting through him like a blade as it echoes along the otherwise empty highway. An endless stream of frantic thoughts floods his mind. *Am I awake? Is this really happening? Where is he? How far behind me is he now? Why isn't he still chasing me? What is he waiting for? Is he gone? Have I made it? Will someone come? Sooner or later someone will come, won't they? A car has to come eventually. And—Carey! What about Carey? Oh God, Carey, where—where is she? Does he have her? Is that why he's given up on me?*

4 MIDNIGHT SOLITAIRE

He stops a moment. Bent over and trying to catch his breath, he looks back at the long stretch of road from which he came. Darkness. Nothing. He begins to remember the attack, the car that seemed to come out of nowhere slamming into theirs, the screams, Carey being dragged off by her hair into the night as if the darkness itself had come alive and taken her, kicking and screaming for help that would never arrive. He recalled falling from the car, dazed and bloodied, his ears ringing, and his vision blurred, and how again the black car had returned, exploding from the darkness and this time striking him. The unimaginable violence of the impact sent him airborne, and he remembers crashing back to the pavement like a ragdoll and laying there looking up at the black sky, wondering if this was where and how he would die. But then he'd remembered Carey, and he knew he had to get up, had to try to help her. He'd struggled to get to his feet, fighting to remain conscious, but by the time he was able to move and regain his bearings, she was gone, her screams no more. And just when he thought he was alone, the silhouette of a man emerged from the darkness, coming toward him with long, purposeful strides, the heels of his boots clacking pavement and the rustling of his long leather duster flapping in the wind. But what he remembers most are the man's eyes, yellow and inhuman, glowing impossibly in the night.

His only memories from there are running, hobbling off as best he could, in shock, in agony and drowning in terror and confusion. What had happened, what *was* happening?

He looks out at the long stretch of road before him. Surely there must be a gas station or motel or something at some point on this godforsaken highway. But he knows he cannot continue on much further. The pain is becoming too great, and he's freezing and starting to shut down from loss of blood and the cold. He straightens up as best he can and wipes the wetness from his eyes.

Something separates from the darkness. But how could...

How did he get in front of me? He—He was behind me, back there in...

The same silhouette, same long strides, but this time the eyes are not glowing, they remain hidden in shadows beneath the flat brim of a western hat. His hands are at his side. In one he holds an enormous knife, the polished steel blade sparkling in the swirl of snow flurries.

He knows this time there is no point in trying to escape. There is no help. He is alone in the middle of nowhere with this man. He will die. Here, in this nightmare, on this lonely stretch of dark highway. And he will never know why.

"Where's my girlfriend?" he asks hopelessly. "What did you do to her?"

The man continues toward him, saying nothing.

"Who are you? Why are you doing this? What the *fuck* is happening!" When he gets no answer he stumbles back a bit, holding his hands up in front of him as if this might somehow achieve something. "Wait, OK—just—you don't have to do this, I didn't do anything to you, I—come on, man, I don't even know you! I'm only twenty-five years old, all right? My name's Martin, my girlfriend's name's Carey and we're getting married soon, I—*please* just *listen* a minute!"

In one fluid motion the man takes the final steps to close the gap between them and slams the huge blade deep into Martin's gut. He holds him steady, clutching him by the throat with one gloved hand while tugging the knife upward with the other, viciously ripping his prey open with a nauseating tearing sound.

The man pulls the knife free, wipes the blade clean on his pants with two long, precise strokes, and then returns it to a scabbard on his belt. Although he never says a word, the man gently cups the back of Martin's head and carefully lays him down on the road. He kneels next to him, positions him as if handling a delicate child, and tenderly strokes Martin's forehead, looking deep into his eyes as he drifts off to another kind of darkness.

The last thing Martin sees are those eyes staring down at him from beneath the brim of that hat. No longer the glowing eyes of a demon, but the sorrowful and compassionate eyes of a human being powerlessly watching him die. In that strange and curiously intimate moment, all of Martin's fears leave him, and he knows that somehow everything will be all right.

He's the lucky one tonight.

6 MIDNIGHT SOLITAIRE

Suddenly, the snow turns to rain.

Night drapes the city and the rain keeps coming down, harder now, lashing the abandoned building and running noisily along the fire escape outside. No thunder or lightning, just the rain…rain and memories…rain and a deck of cards, the same deck of cards he's carried for years now, worn and frayed but still useful.

He sits at a small table in what was once a kitchen, the flames from black ceremonial candles of some kind providing the only light. He pours himself another drink, notices the bottle of vodka is already half empty, and then shuffles the cards and lays them out once again. He checks his watch. Just after midnight. He nods in response to the memory then lets it dissipate like all the rest.

All the while, he plays the game.

It is automatic after all these years, has become second nature to him, something he can play without even focusing on the cards. Solitaire is just another ritual after all, one he often begins without even realizing he's done so.

Sometimes he wins without remembering the moves that got him there, and sometimes even becomes stuck and starts a new game without realizing it. His mind goes elsewhere during his games of midnight solitaire, the repetitive motion causing him to slip into automatic pilot, a trance of sorts, where he loses track of time and place, only to emerge from the game hours later. If nothing else, it helps him teeter between his world and theirs, and passes the night.

The cards aren't falling right, so he scoops them up, gives the deck a final shuffle then sets them aside. He throws back the rest of the vodka and listens to the rhythm of the rain. Staring down into the ice at the bottom of his glass, he takes hold of the bottle and pours himself another. Like most nights, he will continue drinking until the booze leaves him drowsy enough to approach something akin to sleep, though that outcome is still hours away.

In the other room, the remains of the girl—Carey he thinks she said her name was—are on a dirty old mattress he'd found. She didn't understand he'd come to save her, to rescue her, so she died screaming, as they all do, not yet ready to accept that which they need and asked for themselves. He knows their pain, feels it himself. He explained this to her as he skinned and dismembered her then used her blood and bodily fluids to paint the walls, ceilings and floors with his symbols and cyphers, but she chose not to listen. By the time he'd eaten her heart and liver, he'd marked her remains as well, communing with those to whom his offerings are made, those who might one day see fit to rescue him from this sentence he has endured for longer than he cares to remember.

For now he must exist in the world of Man. His world is much older of course, much grander, but he has been away for such a very long time that he sometimes forgets. He has been here since the early times...the first times.

Like so many others before her, Carey told him he was insane, sick and needed help, and while she was right, it didn't make the things he knew to be true any less real. Now she understood, at least to the extent the poor creature ever could, that he had smelled her misery and released her from its chains. In reality, without even realizing it, her death had been her choice, not his. *She* had actually come to *him*. If nothing else, sweet little Carey knows that now, and realizes that sometimes lost souls like hers get exactly what they require, because they are created for very specific purposes.

By the time they find the man out on the highway and his girlfriend here in this condemned building, he will be long gone. Like always, they will release details of the murders and do their best to apprehend him, but the authorities will leave out or downplay the ritualistic aspects of the crimes. Some things are better kept from a smug, weak public. It helps him, and he is grateful to those who will never catch him.

What else can they do or say? Tell people there truly *are* forces in their midst they not only don't fully understand but cannot even begin to control, stop, or in any way prevent or protect them from? Their only choice is to pretend, and then accuse those who disagree with doing the same.

No one intelligent, educated and grounded looks for that which does not exist. They have assured themselves and others that such things are the flights of fancy of the stupid and ignorant, the moronically religious and naively spiritual, the magic-believers and those who think there are still mysteries to this life.

And so, he becomes make-believe. At least until he stands before them and they're wetting their pants, begging for mercy. Then they're not so smug, these children whistling past the graveyards that will soon house their remains.

Confronted with pure evil, there are no believers or skeptics. Only lambs with bowed heads and racing hearts shuffling to slaughter while trying to make sense of things they can never fully comprehend. In the end, they are all make-believe, all there for the catharsis and entertainment of their god.

He rubs his tired eyes, his fingers stained with dried blood. In time the ghostly visions and demonic whispers will fade, as will all else, and he'll fall away into a cradle of alcohol-induced, faithless sleep. But for now he continues to drink hard and fast, tethered to just another ritual, one he despises.

Is he asleep or awake? He can no longer remember.

It doesn't really matter.

Outside, just beyond the grimy windows, the rain keeps on, driving, relentless, and determined to baptize even those things stranded beyond the reach of its salvation.

THREE

D espite the sun, the water is choppy and harsh. An occasional ocean breeze blows up off the canal, cuts through the recreational area with the subtlety of a razor and reminds that while spring is right around the corner, winter has not yet finished its mischief. Despite the chilly temperature there are quite a few walkers and sightseers here today. He takes up position at a picnic table of scarred and aged wood that overlooks the canal. Beyond a guardrail that consists of wooden planks painted white and fastened to cement posts, Doc watches the paved lane below. Narrow, like a sidewalk, a handful of people stroll, jog, power-walk, bicycle and rollerblade on it, coming and going along the cement path, hurrying as if to sneak in a quick visit before winter gives them all one last kick in the ass. Others stand watching the water, doing their best to enjoy the view on a sunny but brisk Sunday morning.

On the far side of the canal an identical paved path runs the length of the water. Bicyclers and such move along it as well, made smaller by the distance. Above them are thick woods along the incline of land that rises up to meet a crystal blue skyline. Scattered throughout, a few expensive homes are barely visible through the forest; the kind wealthy people live in, with flagpoles out front flying the stars and stripes alongside those belonging to local yacht clubs.

To his left, in the distance, the Sagamore Bridge extends over the canal, connecting Cape Cod to the mainland. With its enormous arched and open steel top, the bridge reminds Doc of the skeletal remains of a giant creature that died while spanning both shores, its carcass frozen in place and long since reduced to bone. Traffic is unusually light in both directions, even for this time of year.

He is suddenly distracted by a blur of white. A seagull lands on the railing not far from his table and stares at him as if trying desperately to communicate. Doc watches the bird's small, attentive eye, hoping to hear him, to understand. The seagull hops down and walks along the grass, so close he's within Doc's reach. After another staring session, the seagull hops back up on the railing. In an attempt to fathom what the creature is trying to convey, Doc continues to study the bird and opens his mind to the possibilities, but a woman walking past startles it, and the seagull flies away.

He watches it soar toward the bridge, carried off on the breeze high above the waves, over the boats and trees. Wonder gives way to envy.

A thickly built middle-aged man of average height, Doc Banta dresses like a character straight out of 1950s film noir: black suit, white shirt, skinny black tie, black wingtips. Slicked straight back, his silver hair is thick for a man his age, nearly reaches his shoulders and contrasts nicely with his olive skin. Dark wayfarers rest on his hawkish nose, concealing icy blue eyes. Even his car, a cherry 1957 two-door Bel Air hardtop, looks like something out of an old movie.

He digs a pack of unfiltered Pall Malls from his inside jacket pocket, sparks one up with his Zippo and scratches absently at the salt-and-pepper stubble on his face.

"Do you still feel me?" he quietly asks the air, the water, the trees, knowing one day he will once again look eye-to-eye with the ones he truly wants to ask. "Do you still feel my love?" For now the hatred drives him, as it has for some time, and for now that's enough. It's all rehearsal for the showdown, a final confrontation of horrific violence he cannot escape. *For now,* Doc thinks, *listen to the wind and you'll hear them whispering in answer.*

He missed the bastard by mere days, but over the last several months he's been getting closer. It's only a matter of time. The last victim, a young woman and her boyfriend, were killed not far from here. A local news station did a story on them. It said the young woman, Carey Sinclair her name was, often came to the canal to rollerblade. It was one of her favorite spots. Remembering the photographs he's seen of her and her boyfriend, Doc tries to imagine her here along with him. In a way she is. On a vast stretch of Cape Cod highway, on the far side of the bridge perhaps five minutes from here, The Dealer drove them off the road, killed her boyfriend and kidnapped Carey. Gutted the poor bastard, left him for dead in the street. Didn't want him, didn't need him. The Dealer had come for the girl. The newspapers say he'd taken her back across the bridge to the mainland, all the way to some abandoned shithole he'd found in Brockton, a small city nearly an hour away. There, he'd done his work and performed his rituals on a helpless twenty-three-year-old kid. Just thinking about it, remembering back, knowing what it's like, what the parents and loved ones of those two kids are feeling, what they'll feel for the rest of their lives makes Doc's blood boil. The authorities posture publicly, like they always do, but nothing will come of it. The Dealer's long gone, same as always.

But Doc knows where he's headed, because he's headed there too.

An enormous SUV pulls up into a nearby parking space. A man in his forties gets out, accompanied by a teenage girl. To the casual observer it would appear that Doc hasn't even noticed. But he misses nothing, takes it all in without once turning his head. The man, in a blue sweat suit with white stripes, stops to tie the laces on his Nike high-tops then adjusts his freshly dyed hair. He's one of those middle-aged guys who makes online profiles and lists his age as twenty-nine even though it's really forty-six. The kind who dresses like the star of an old Run-DMC video and thinks teenage girls find him irresistibly cool rather than laughable. The kind who calls every female he encounters *hon.*

The girl, probably his daughter, is reed thin and no more than fourteen or fifteen. Her coat hangs open to reveal a low-cut blouse and cleavage clearly enhanced by a pushup bra. Her jeans are so tight they appear to have been spray-painted on. In a pair of brown UGG boots, she skip-walks to the railing and looks out over the water. Her makeup is too heavy for a girl her age, applied with the intent of making her appear older, but only serves to showcase a young girl desperately trying to appear sexy and worldly and failing miserably at both.

It isn't until the man joins her at the railing, slinks his arms around her from behind and pulls her close that Doc realizes this is not his daughter after all.

At least he hopes not.

Doc smokes his cigarette, stares at the ocean and pretends to ignore the giggling and grope-fest happening less than ten feet from where he stands. The girl is trying, that much is obvious. But it's also clear that just beneath her studied exterior, there lurks an awkward and uncertain little girl with virtually no self-esteem struggling to find her identity and thinking maybe she's found it in the creep in the tracksuit.

"Be right back baby," the man says, pointing to a small building further down the lot that houses a public bathroom. "Need to drain the main vein."

The girl gives an obligatory laugh then turns back to the canal as the man struts towards the restrooms.

Doc holds his ground. By the time he's finished his cigarette, dropped it to the pavement and crushed it beneath his shoe, the man has vanished into the building and he is alone with the girl. He turns, looks directly at her. She seems to sense his eyes on her and glances nervously over her shoulder at him. She smiles. *Hey*, she says. Doc nods but says nothing, just stares at her, his wayfarers masking his eyes.

"What?" she says defensively.

"How old are you?"

"How old are *you*?"

"Forty-nine."

"Wow, you're older than my dad."

"How about your boyfriend, is he older than your dad?"

"Jackie?" she laughs and shakes her head. "He's not my boyfriend."

Doc says nothing.

"It's none of your business," she tells him.

Doc looks back out at the water.

"Besides," she says, "I'm nineteen."

"Try again."

"What do you care?"

"I had a daughter once."

"So?"

"She would've been right around your age."

The girl smiles in a manner she thinks is seductive, leans against the railing and folds her arms across her chest. "What's my age?"

"Fifteen."

"Sixteen," she says defiantly, and then, realizing he hasn't bought it, adds, "Well, in a month and a half anyways."

"Got a cellphone?" Doc asks.

The girl blanches, clearly offended. "Ah, *duh*," she says, holding up an iPhone as if in evidence.

"Call somebody to come pick you up."

This worries her, and the smirk on her face fades. "Why?"

Doc turns and walks along the narrow sidewalk to the restrooms. He can feel the girl watching as he goes, but she doesn't follow or say a word. By the time he's reached the door, Doc hears whistling.

The interior of the men's room is relatively clean and empty, but for whistling Jackie, who has finished his business and taken up position in front of a large mirror. He inspects himself and smiles wide, pointing at his reflection with both hands. "Hell yeah, my man, that's what I'm talking about!"

Doc stands just inside the doorway. He removes his sunglasses, folds them closed and slides them into his jacket pocket.

"How's it going?" Jackie says, moving toward the door, and then, realizing Doc has no intention of moving, hesitates and smiles nervously. "Excuse me."

Doc doesn't move.

"Want to let me by, chief?" Jackie says, chuckling as if they're old friends. He reeks of sweet, cheap cologne. Very slowly, Doc shakes his head no.

Jackie grins at him like the fool he is. "What's the problem, pal? Just want to get by, OK?"

"That girl out there," he says evenly.

"Yeah, what about her?"

"She's fifteen years old."

"What are you, a cop?" He clears his throat, puffs up his chest and shuffles about, nervously rubbing at his nose. "Relax, all right? I'm her soccer coach, I know her parents. She's got a tough home life and I'm just trying to help her out." He manages to find some of his swagger back, straightens his posture and squares his stance. "And frankly, I'm offended by what you're inferring, *bud*. I'm a married man with kids of my own. I'm just trying to mentor and befriend a kid in need here."

"By feeling her up?"

Jackie's face flushes. "What? I didn't—I didn't do that, I just hugged—you mean just now out there? How dare you! I gave her a hug, for Christ's sake, nothing—who the fuck are you to hassle me anyway? Get the hell out of my way, man. This is bullshit. I don't have to stand here and listen to this. I don't know you and you don't know me, right? So fuck off before you get hurt, *pops*."

Five minutes later Doc is back on the highway, headed out of state and back to business. He has a long drive, and The Dealer is already ahead of him, already on the move. There's no time to waste.

Miles back, in a restroom near the Cape Cod Canal, a soccer coach with a penchant for teenage girls named Jackie Hunt lies on the cold tile floor in a pool of his own blood, urine, shit and teeth. Blubbering, he holds what remains of his nose in place in the hopes that once he gets to the emergency room they might be able to save it.

Stone-faced, Doc drives on like the old road dog he's become, lets the memory slip and blow away along the highway like the rest in his wake and slides *The Best of Robert Johnson* into the CD player. Quickly lost in the scratchy old blues recordings of haunting guitar riffs, Johnson's ethereal voice sings to him from the past about devils on his heels, luring him to another place and time, even if just for a short while, where none of this matters.

FOUR

R ain pours across the windshield in a steady thick stream, and despite the rapid sweep of wipers, the continuous watery veil makes visibility all but impossible. Though only late afternoon, the dark skies and heavy rains make it feel more like the middle of the night, especially out on the open road. *Strangest damn weather this time of year,* she thinks. *Sunny and still one minute, pouring rain the next, snowing the next.* The radio station with the 80s retro format she's been listening to fades in and out, losing strength the farther Greer drives, and she's not seen oncoming headlights or even any behind her in more than twenty minutes. She hits the SCAN button on the FM tuner in the hopes of locking on a signal strong enough to tune in, but the digital numbers tumble one into the next, spanning the dial again and again. Looming in the distance is a row of huge high-tension towers, metal giants standing in the dark rain like otherworldly shrines left behind by an ancient alien culture. *That explains it,* she thinks, switching off the tuner. She knows she's somewhere near the western part of the state, but Greer isn't familiar with these back roads. She's been damn near everywhere in her thirty-seven years—all over the United States and into select areas of Canada and Mexico—but she's a flyer. For years she's jetted into a locale, conducted business in hotels, restaurants or boardrooms, at conventions or the occasional tradeshow, then hopped another flight to wherever else the company has her going. *I've been everywhere,* she often jokes, *but only to their hotels, restaurants and airports.* Now, like everything else, it doesn't seem as fun as it once did. No, that's the wrong word. It was never fun. She moved through her life like a spectator, conducting it in ways she'd become accustomed to, but in recent months what was once automatic-pilot-doable has become unbearable. A life where numbers and sales and clients and schedules and product took the place of friends, family, love and a real life had never been her dream, was never part of the plan. Yet here she is. The occasional one-night stands on the road, the loneliness, a life of impersonal and surface interactions with people she barely knows and will probably never see again, the fear of waking up one day and realizing who she's really become, what she's really done with her so-called life and how she's wasted much of it as a salesperson, bopping from state to state, client to client, city to city, making money, kicking ass and taking names. That's Greer Fields, a machine. That's what her colleagues have called her for years, a machine in a skirt-suit and heels that can close a client before they even know she's worked them. And now she's little more than a ghost in her own haunted life. She has no family, no relationship and few friends. Decades before there was a husband—the one true love of her life—but her career on the road killed that within a year. She's never looked back. At least that's what she tells herself when she's alone in the dark, drunk and full of regret. A few boyfriends—even a girlfriend briefly once—but nothing of any real import or value. Like everything else in her life, relationships are transitory, and her constant motion leaves little time to worry about it, think about it or change it. There is her apartment in Boston, a beautiful and elegant space with a great view that others can only dream about. There is her car, the Audi—a new one every three years—a closet full of clothes, jewelry, nice things, and with no husband, no kids and no mortgage, a great portfolio with a huge retirement fund. Not too shabby for an orphan raised in foster homes who had to scratch and claw her way to anything even remotely resembling happiness. And yet, possessions, six-figure salary and all, she's miserable. Alone, lost, drifting closer and closer to forty with each passing day and still with no clue as to how she might escape this life before she becomes that grizzled old alcoholic seller she's seen on the road for years, hanging out in airport bars, her best days reduced to vague memories, struggling to hang on and get by while trying to compete with younger, sexier, smarter, quicker, better salespeople who every year take just a little bit more of her life, her livelihood, her turf, her soul. A pathetic used-to-be powerbroker reduced to telling stories at diners to other drunks and losers at one in the morning in the middle of fucking nowhere.

Alone. That's how she lives and how she believes she'll die unless she changes things now. Which is precisely why she's finally listened to that nagging voice in her head, done what's she's done, and literally walked away from her life, her job, responsibilities and commitments.

Where am I supposed to go?

Pack a bag, get in the car and do it.

How will I know where to go?

You don't have to know. I know.

But—

I know.

The first day she got all of twenty minutes from her apartment in Boston and took a room at a hotel to think things through and make sure this was really the move she wanted to make. Earlier that day she'd been sitting nude on the edge of a bed, staring at the walls and thinking, *one more goddamn hotel.* She'd glanced at her reflection in the mirrored closet door on the far side of the room and figured if nothing else she was still in good shape physically. Years of working out in hotel gyms, never having had children and a blessed metabolism had all worked in her favor on that count. At five-six and one hundred and twenty-five pounds she essentially still has the body she'd possessed in her twenties. *And so what?* By morning—this morning—she decides to continue on. She has no choice. Whatever's out there waiting for her has to be better than what she's leaving behind. And if not, then so be it.

Destiny makes no promises. Bitch.

Memories of the hotel room blur as the rain sluicing along the windshield swallows them whole, sweeps them away with the wipers until all that remains is a dark and empty highway. On the passenger seat Greer's iPhone vibrates and hums, indicating someone has left yet another voicemail for her. Without looking she reaches over, silences it and drives on. Last check she already had over twenty messages. Certainly understandable, as this is so unlike her. A lot of people at work have surely already begun to panic and assume the worst; that something awful has happened to her. The Machine is always on time, always at work, always ready for the next trip, always leading the pack in sales and balls and attitude. That's all she has. It's become her entire life. But now it's the same as the road rolling away in the rearview. Gone.

Now, she thinks, *I really am a ghost.*

She blows a renegade strand of brown hair up out of her eyes, runs a hand through her relatively short hair and sighs. Are these suicidal thoughts she's feeling or just the fear and anxiety of uncertainty and loss of control?

She doesn't want to die. Does she?

Before she can think any more about it, Greer sees the flames.

Surreal and impossible in the pouring rain, yet there they are on the side of the road, great flickering tongues of fire rumbling and bursting, rising up and reaching for the gray sky. She slows the car a bit as she gets closer and realizes the flames have engulfed and originate from a car in the breakdown lane.

She reaches for her phone, eyes squinting through the rain. *Christ, where's the driver, the passengers? Are they still inside?*

Greer pulls over into the breakdown lane perhaps fifty yards from the burning car, careful not to get too close in case the gas tank ignites, if it hasn't already. Without taking her eyes from the wreckage, she grips her phone and presses 911.

The line crackles. Reception is horrid, but she can make out ringing on the other end of the line.

"9-1-1," a faint female voice answers, "what is your emergency?"

Greer explains. The operator asks for her name and location, tells her to stay clear of the burning car, asks if there is anyone trapped in the vehicle, the make and model of the vehicle, and if there is anyone else on the scene.

"Just me," Greer says, glancing at the rearview before returning her eyes to the car. "And there doesn't appear to be anyone inside, but I can't be certain."

"I'm dispatching fire and rescue to your location now," the operator tells her. "We'd like you to stay on-scene please, as the police may need to take a witness statement."

"I didn't witness anything. I simply happened upon this and reported it."

"I understand, ma'am, however—"

"I'm sorry, but I'm late for an appointment and this rain is slowing me down as it is. I have nothing to do with this and nothing more to add. You have my name and information, should the authorities need to speak with me I'll be happy to talk with them via phone or at some later, more convenient date." Greer hangs up without waiting for a response and tosses the phone back onto the passenger seat. Craning her neck for a better view, she slowly pulls out onto the highway, slinking by the fiery vehicle, a relatively new black Dodge Charger.

The rain has extinguished some of the flames, but the fire continues to rage. Although the vehicle appears to be empty, Greer notices an overturned can of gasoline that's been tossed on the side of the road not far from the car.

Damn. Somebody torched it.

She accelerates, leaves the inferno in her rearview.

A mile or so later she sees something trudging through the rain along the side of the road. When she gets closer she realizes it's a man walking in the breakdown lane. Dressed in a long dark duster, boots and a flat-brimmed western hat, a large leather knapsack slung over his shoulder, he looks oddly out of place on the side of a highway in western Massachusetts.

Greer slows the car.

The man turns, looks back over his shoulder.

Unsure why, Greer immediately feels mesmerized and is unable to take her eyes from him.

Ruggedly handsome, he appears to be about her age—somewhere in his middle to late thirties—a big man, six-three or four and well over two hundred pounds. But he's not heavy, he's in shape and looks like the sort of individual that can handle himself, and probably does on a regular basis.

As her headlights catch his eyes they glow yellow like an animal's, and very slowly, the man sticks his hand out, extends a thumb and smiles at her.

Greer has already started to pull over when she blinks rapidly and breaks the spell. Realizing what she's doing, she turns back onto the highway and hits the gas, surging off into the storm until the man is little more than a dark smudge in the distance.

20 MIDNIGHT SOLITAIRE

Miles later, for reasons she cannot yet understand, she is still trembling.

FIVE

In the pouring rain, a man sits alone on a deserted playground. Slumped on a canvas swing that dangles from a chain on an old iron swing set, his feet are stretched out before him and he clutches a Styrofoam cup of coffee in both hands. He remains stationary, his head bowed, as if something on the ground before him has captured his attention. Occasionally, he raises the cup to his mouth and sips the coffee, but otherwise he is still, seemingly oblivious to the weather, huddled in a long dark raincoat, a black knit hat pulled down over his ears.

Sometimes Luke Thompson goes to parks or playgrounds to think. Sometimes he goes for the sole purpose of watching children play. There is nothing profound about the former, nothing nefarious about the latter. He simply likes children. He has no children of his own but sometimes thinks if he did he could at least point to one positive accomplishment in what has otherwise been a useless life. He is a failure as a man and a husband—he knows that—and although he fantasizes about being a good father, he understands he'd more than likely fail at that as well. Rachel has every right to suggest this, to fear it. She has tried so hard, believed in him when no one else did and when he didn't deserve it. And he's let her down every time. Though he knows it will never happen, Luke still clings now and then to the fantasy that perhaps one day he and Rachel will be able to sort things out and get it all back to the way it once was. The way it was early on. Those days were so short-lived he sometimes wonders if they ever really happened at all. Either way, if he could just get it back he knows they'd be happy and have a family...*be* a family. It's all he's ever really wanted. Yet it remains just beyond his reach. Always has. Always will.

Of course watching other people's children frolic is a poor substitute, but it affords him the chance to live vicariously through the parents, those who gather in small clusters at the fringes of parks and playgrounds, most showing less interest in the play of their own children than he does. They have no idea how lucky they are. That's the worst part of being without children, he thinks. Never having the chance to live those little moments, those mundane everyday situations and conversations and experiences so many take for granted. They're so fortunate, these parents, but so few seem to realize it. He can't very well blame them, though. He certainly didn't have much better. In fact, he had far worse. He's only learned to cherish his life now that he's lost it and will never again have the chance to make it what he's always dreamed it could be.

Luke may as well have been born with a gun in his hand and a prison number stenciled across his chest. Just like the old man and his old man before him, one more criminal in a line of many. *Bad company*, his father used to call it. *That's what we are, boy, bad company. And that's all we'll ever be.*

Just like the beatings he'd endured as a kid, the fallout from his old man's words continues to linger, sticking to him like a second skin. He had his chance with Rachel, and he blew it.

He sits in the rain and remembers the last day he saw her. More than a week of driving and wandering, trying to figure out what to do and where to go next, he stops only when the driving becomes too much, and he can no longer put off sleep. Then it's off the highway, into one of these little towns, hit a convenience store or something easy, grab some fast cash then back on the road before anyone knows what's happened. Find another roadside motel and spend the night with a bottle, maybe a local working girl if he gets lucky or the score's enough to cover it. Then right back out on the road to...what? Does it even matter anymore? Has it ever?

His memory is nothing special, but for some reason whenever he pulls a job he remembers everything in vivid detail. It's always been this way, all his life. The jobs replay in his head for days, sometimes weeks, crystal clear like he's watching a movie. On this dark and dreary late afternoon he remembers the last job, a liquor store he knocked over the night before. The cashier, a twenty-something woman wearing a bandana, gobs of eye makeup, big silver hoop earrings, too-tight jeans and a sweatshirt with a depiction of a kitten holding a shotgun beneath the caption: *A Little Pussy Never Hurt Anyone*, freaks out the moment he walks through the door. Like people sometimes do when a man like Luke Thompson pulls a ski mask down over his face, raids their space and points a gun at them, she immediately begins pleading with him and reeling off her life's story. For example, within thirty seconds or so, Luke knows the woman has two children, that her boyfriend lost his job and is struggling with a drinking problem, and that she's holding down two jobs and going to college online on her nights off and doesn't need this shit in her life and just take the money or whatever you want because I seriously—*seriously*—do not give a fuck, just please don't hurt me.

Luke thrusts a small canvas bag at her, and in his fiercest voice orders her to fill it with the money from the register fast as she can, or he'll blow her head off. *You ever want to see your kids again you better hurry the fuck up.*

He remembers her stuffing the bag with cash, her heavy breasts shifting beneath the sweatshirt, the kitten with the shotgun rippling and dancing as her eye makeup runs, diluted by tears, across her cheeks in black swathes. He also remembers the guilt. He despises robbing women.

Wrong place, wrong time. Nothing personal.

Once the bag is full he takes a quick peek over his shoulder at the parking lot. Satisfied it's empty he waves the gun at the camera over the counter and demands the surveillance tape. Trembling, the woman ejects the cassette from the recorder under the counter and hands it over.

Stop crying. He stuffs the tape in the bag, quickly counts out a hundred in twenties from the stash she's just given him then tosses them on the counter. *Put that in your purse. Buy your kids something. Nobody's gonna know.*

Are you serious?

As he leaves, fear becomes confusion, and then amusement.

Memories of the woman scooping up the money morphs into visions of Rachel standing at the foot of the bed glaring at him. Their apartment, rundown and in need of a good cleaning, and Rachel dressed for work, doing her best, trying to hold a secretarial job while Luke did what he does, works the angles, tries to secure a decent score, always so close to that big one that will change their lives and make everything all right. A weary knight in armor tarnished and dented, chasing dragons that don't exist, a holy grail destined to remain cloaked in the fog of dreams just beyond the grasp of anything real, his is a doomed crusade. And he knows it. Deep down he always has.

But now Rachel knows it too, and she has lost her faith. It's gone and taken with it any chance Luke has at redemption.

You had a chance at a straight life, and you couldn't do it.

He watches the puddles at his feet, sees his reflection in them staring back at him with dead, empty eyes.

You couldn't hold a regular job. I work my ass off, and we have nothing.

Rachel, I—

It's over. I'm done. I mean it. I'm too old for this.

I can fix it, just give me a chance to make it right and I will.

You've had five years to make it right. You're thirty-years-old and you're still running around like some punk. You'll be back in prison in no time. And I can't do it again. I can't—I won't—wait for you again. I'm done. I love you, but I'm done.

He closes his eyes. She holds her arm up so he can see her bare wrist.

Where's my watch? You pawned it, didn't you? You gambled it away, right? You gave me that for our anniversary. What's it worth? Fifty bucks? It meant more to me than that. I thought it meant more to you too. And you want me to get pregnant. You expect me to bring a child into this mess?

Let me explain, I—

I've been listening to your explanations for years. No more.

Rachel, I love you, baby, don't—

You don't love me. You don't love anybody. You don't know how.

Her face lingers there behind his eyes. Broken.

When I get home from work I'm leaving. I mean it this time.

Until the moment came when she walked out with a suitcase in hand, he didn't believe she'd really go through with it.

Now, in the rain, far from home, he knows there is no going back, no more chances. His life—Rachel—is gone. None of it's coming back. He started off in New York and has gotten as far as Western Massachusetts. Maybe he'll swing up into New Hampshire then Maine, maybe even slip into Canada.

Doesn't matter. The last leg has arrived, and he knows this. It's not about whether or not he'll go out, it's down to how. As a child Luke was in and out of juvenile detention centers. As an adult he's done numerous stretches in county jails and two stretches in state prisons, one of three years, the other sixteen months. But he has not been incarcerated in more than three years now. Still, Rachel is right. It's only a matter of time. Before, when he still had something to go home to—and a home at all for that matter—there was always the hope that once he did his time and got back into Rachel's arms everything would be all right, he could straighten things out and finally do the right thing. But there was no point now. It was over. Only this time, he had no intention of going back to prison. Luke Thompson would never be locked up in anything again, other than the coffin they buried him in.

Go out swinging, his old man used to say. *Never lie down for nobody. Go out fighting with everything you got.*

But he is not his father. He may not be much better, but he refuses to be that bad. Luke is violent if he has to be. His father was violent because he enjoyed it, as any sadist does. Luke is a thief, no more, no less.

Still, maybe the old man was right. Even if he wasn't, Luke knows he will follow that last bit of advice. Either he will find his way and by some miracle get a life worth living back, or he will die fighting and kicking his way out of this world like his father before him. Regardless, this ghost he's become, this phantom aimlessly traveling back roads and highways, is not long for this world.

That Luke Thompson is going to die. One way or the other.

He takes another swallow of coffee then tosses the cup aside, watching as the remains spill and trickle into the dirty puddles at his feet.

The rain falls in diagonal sheets, pummeling and crashing down on him with a vengeance. It consumes him, distorts his presence to a mere silhouette in the intensifying storm.

He remains frozen, helpless.

As if he no longer exists. As if he never really has.

SIX

The Moonlight Road Motor Inn, a relic left over from before the interstate was built, sits in partial light, set back a ways from the two-lane highway in the middle of a cracked patch of pavement, its sign—a yellow half-moon with a human face winking out at the road—buzzes and blinks in the heavy downpour. The main office is all angles, glass and pitched roof, and looks like something built in the 1950s, which it was. The units, thirty in all, are housed in one long, narrow, single-story rectangle of a building set on a large dirt lot perhaps thirty yards to the right of the office. Were one to drive by while the sign was off, one might mistake The Moonlight Road Motor Inn long closed and abandoned, as the upkeep has been less than meticulous in recent years. It is a dying building on a rural highway in a part of Massachusetts that is largely farmland and open, unoccupied space.

The last stop in the middle of nowhere, Kit Piper thinks. *Perfect.*

Slumped in the front seat of her dilapidated 1990 Honda Civic while smoking the last of a blunt, she focuses on a golf-ball-size crystal at the end of a cheap chain dangling from the rearview mirror. A trinket she picked up at a New Age kiosk in Springfield a few months before, until recently it held no real meaning to her, Kit just thinks it's pretty and likes the way it catches the moonlight, particularly when she's stoned.

A news report drones from the tinny car speakers, an announcer going on and on about the rainstorms marching through the area and how they're being followed by a major band of snow and ice that will arrive later this evening. *Probably the last snow of the season*, she thinks. Winter never goes out easy.

Kit finishes the blunt, tosses the roach in the ashtray and quickly flips through her manuscript pages. Hopefully somewhere in this mess there's a novel, but who knows? She's been working on it for more than a year and she still has no idea what the hell it's about. She skims the last chapter, hates everything she reads and jams the manuscript along with her laptop into a worn knapsack. Maybe later tonight, once Carlin Pelham (the man she relives each night) has gone home and it's quiet, she can get some work done on it. She removes her black, plastic frame glasses and rubs her eyes. She's had some shit jobs in her twenty-six years, and while working the night desk at this dump sucks, it's not as bad as waiting tables or struggling through some office gig. At least here she's primarily by herself and has time to write. The money's horrible, just a touch over minimum wage, but her expenses aren't too bad now that she's living at home again. After a stint in New York City, she realized being on her own wasn't going to be as easy as she'd imagined, and after running into trouble, she moved back home with her mother. There is a great deal of love between them, but theirs has always been a somewhat contentious relationship. She hopes it's only temporary, and that soon she'll have enough money saved and get enough writing done so she can pack up and give the Big Apple another try.

Writing is such a long shot, her mother constantly warns. *You've always been a daydreamer, but why not pursue something more solid and less creative?*

A few more months, she thinks, replacing her eyeglasses, *and none of this will matter. One way or another, I'll be free.*

With a sigh, Kit looks out the window at the rain pounding the highway and turning the dirt lot to a muddy mess. But for her Honda, Carlin's Chevy van and two cars parked in front of the units, both lots are empty. The large glass panels along the front of the office are blurred by the storm, but the light within reveals Carlin's distorted figure sitting behind the front desk, fiddling with his laptop.

According to Kit's watch, the start of her shift is still ten minutes away, but Carlin probably wants to get home before the snow starts and things get really bad. While he doesn't deserve her generosity, she decides to offer it anyway. She figures she owes him since he has no idea she'll be using him in her novel at some point. Can't pass up a character that good. Kit pops a mint, grabs her knapsack, pulls her ratty old Army jacket in tight around her and makes a mad dash for the office.

The rain batters her, cold and relentless, her Doc Martens boots splashing puddles as she goes.

A moment later she stumbles through the front door, closes it behind her then leans back against it. Dripping and out of breath, Kit pulls her hat off, tucks it in the knapsack and waits for Carlin to acknowledge her with his usual, wildly inappropriate banter.

He glances up over the top of his laptop. "Breathing heavy and soaking wet, just the way I like you. What's up Nipples?"

"Really? You're just going to keep right on calling me that, huh?"

"You love it."

"No, actually, I don't."

"Hey, you come waltzing in here the other night blasting those things through your shirt, what do you expect?"

"It was cold, I—OK, you know what, I am not having this conversation with you again."

"Hey, you call me *Asshole*."

"But you are an asshole, Carlin."

"And you got great nipples, everybody wins." He points a stubby finger at her. "I'm telling you, girl, we should party naked. I'll rock your world."

"Awesome, I totally just threw up in my mouth." Kit pushes away from the door and looks back out at the night. "Unbelievable out there."

"Only gonna get worse," Carlin says, returning his attention to the laptop. "Got a bad snowstorm coming. That's what the honey on channel four said anyway. You might get a straggler or two tonight, but I doubt it. It's been dead."

She motions to the units with her chin. "Couple sleepers?"

"A single in fourteen, businessman-type, and a double in ten, a couple a few years younger than you. Total fuck bunnies."

Doing her best to ignore the porn playing on Carlin's laptop, Kit slips into the office behind the counter. A cramped and mussed area, it smells like perspiration and old milk. On the desk, amidst stacks of paperwork, are a partially eaten carton of Chinese food and the annihilated remains of a box of Twinkies.

Kit throws her coat over the back of the desk chair, sets her knapsack down then rejoins Carlin out front.

A plump little man with a penchant for ratty sweatpants and sweaters two sizes too small for him, Carlin Pelham is fifty-three, and but for an unkempt horseshoe around the lower portion of his head, completely bald. He always looks like he needs a shave and smells like he could use a good head-to-toe scrubbing. His skin is pasty and unhealthy looking, and when he breathes he tends to wheeze and sniffle incessantly. Luckily for Carlin, his uncle owns the motel, or he'd have been fired long ago. Carlin lives in a small house a few miles from the motel with Marty, his wife of twenty-five years. She's on disability for severe depression and agoraphobia, is nearly five hundred pounds and has not left their home in more than eight years. Kit has only seen her in photographs.

Had she not spoken to her on the phone a few times when Carlin hadn't gone straight home after his shift and she'd called looking for him, Kit probably wouldn't believe she existed.

Although Kit has worked with Carlin for several months now, they only see each other for short intervals as they change shifts. Still, due to Carlin's shocking lack of hygiene, his pornography addiction, breathtaking lack of social skills and his general disregard for anything even remotely resembling sexual harassment laws, her interactions with him are almost always memorable.

"So you want me to stay?" Carlin asks, bouncing his eyebrows. "If it gets bad maybe we'll get snowed in together. Power could go out. No power, no heat. You see where I'm going with this?"

"One, gross." Kit piles her jet-black hair atop her head and holds it in place with a plastic clip. "And two, you need to get home to Marty. Remember Marty, your *wife*?"

"She's sleeping by now," he says softly. "Don't even know I'm gone."

Despite the fact that Carlin is, well, *Carlin*, she can't help but feel a bit sorry for him. This is his life. It isn't going to change or improve. Ever. At least for Kit this is a temporary setback. She still has her whole life ahead of her.

But then, like any character in this novel that is life, can she be sure?

"I bet she's already worrying about you getting home safely," Kit tells him.

He shrugs. "Maybe."

The woman in the video does a cartoon orgasm scream in time with the man slamming into her from behind. "Could you shut that off?"

"Don't act like you don't like it." He grins, points to the screen. "If I had a crank that big I'd rule the world."

"Yeah. Not so much."

He shuts the laptop, silences the silicone blonde screamer. "Anyway, drawer's balanced. Joe Business paid with a Visa, but the other dude paid cash. Ice machine's full and I put the number for the plow guys on the bulletin board in case you need them come morning. If plows can even get through, that is."

"Thanks, Carlin. That was actually nice of you."

"No problem." He slides down out of his chair, grabs his plaid flannel coat from the office then scoops up his laptop and tucks it under his arm. "But if you had any class at all you'd show me how grateful you are."

"Not to diminish your status as the grandmaster connoisseur of class, but you did something kind without any ulterior motives. Don't ruin it."

Carlin pulls a fur hat with earflaps from his coat pocket and slaps it on his head. "Tell you what. Flash your tits and we'll call it even."

"OK, drive safely now." Kit takes up position on the chair he just vacated and slides her knapsack onto the counter. "Or not."

"Fine, you win, a hand-job it is."

"Yeah, just not feeling the whole Elmer Fudd fetish tonight, dude, sorry."

Chuckling, he stops at the front door and gazes out at the rain. "Black as coal out there tonight."

"That's what happens when the sun goes down, Carlin. It's called darkness."

Normally he'd have a quick comeback, but this time says nothing and continues staring out at the parking lot. Kit removes her manuscript pages from the knapsack, drops them on the counter then notices he's still standing there quietly. "Carlin? You OK?"

With his back to her, he nods.

"What is it?" she asks.

"I don't know," he answers a moment later, his voice unusually serious. "Just got a weird feeling there for a second."

"Great, I have to work here the rest of the night by myself, thanks for freaking me out. A weird feeling about what?"

He turns, looks back at her. There is something in Carlin Pelham's face Kit has never seen before. Not quite fear, but something similar.

"Carlin?" Kit presses.

"It's nothing, I'm just tired. Whole lot of nothing out there, like always. That's why I like days. Kind of creepy here at night sometimes."

"Tell me about it."

"Catch you tomorrow." He grabs the door and pushes it open, letting in the cold air and a spray of rain. "Have a good night, Nipples."

"You too, Asshole."

Kit watches him go, the door slowly closing behind him on its delayed spring. When he reaches his van at the edge of the paved portion of the lot, Kit returns her attention to her novel.

As Carlin rounds the rear of his van he notices someone standing in the shadows to his left. He stops, one hand on the van door. "Who's that over there?" he calls above the pouring rain.

A man. A large man in a cowboy hat and a duster.

Without taking his eyes from him, Carlin pulls open the van door, places his computer on the seat then casually searches next to it for the ax handle he keeps there. "Can I help you, buddy?"

The man steps closer but he still can't make out his eyes, shielded beneath the flat brim of his hat.

"What the hell you doing out here?" Carlin asks. "You need some help?"

Rain runs off the roof of the motel, through the gutters and along the lot, gushing and trickling as the man shrugs off his duster. It falls to the ground with a thud, and for the first time Carlin realizes the size of this man, because he is shirtless. His body is chiseled and slick in the rain. It is also crisscrossed and littered with scars indicating this man has been stabbed, slashed and even shot numerous times. On the inside of each forearm are tattoos representing playing cards. On the left, the Ace of Spades. On the right, the Ace of Hearts. The man holds his arms out on either side of him and slowly curls his hands into fists, accentuating the network of thick veins that run along his flesh.

Carlin finds the ax handle, grips it tight and holds it down by his side; hopeful the man hasn't seen it. He can't decide if he should hop in the van and lock the door or run for the office. *Probably won't make either one*, he thinks. "What are you doing?" Carlin asks, doing his best to disguise the fear in his voice. "This is private property, OK? Get out of here or I'll call the cops."

The man turns, shows him his back. In three fanned out rows, the remainder of the deck of cards are tattooed across the man's broad back, bright and colorful amidst another battlefield of scars. He raises his head, looks to the sky, the rain, arms held out wider still as if summoning some greater force from the heavens above.

Carlin decides that since the man has turned his back he has a chance. He could get in the van and get away, but what about Kit? He can't just leave her here. Even if he called for help he—*help, you stupid bastard, call for help!*

Hand shaking, he reaches into his coat pocket for his cellphone.

Before he can press the screen the man spins back around, and this time Carlin can see his eyes. He wishes now he couldn't. He wishes he never sees anything like them again, unaware that he will see nothing but those demonic eyes peering down at him for all eternity.

"*Please*," Carlin whispers. It's all he can muster. Even as his bladder lets go and he pees himself, he cannot move or summon another word. He simply stands there trembling. The phone drops to the pavement.

The man pulls a knife from the back of his pants, turning the blade slowly, seductively. It is the largest knife Carlin has ever seen.

Carlin feebly raises the ax handle, but he's so scared and shaking so badly he can't hold it still. He thinks about Marty. Who'll take care of her?

As the blade is thrust up and under his ribcage, Carlin screams. But it quickly becomes a gurgling gasp as blood and bile explode up out of his throat and into his mouth. The man wraps his free arm around him and gently lowers him to the pavement on his back, ripping the knife up then pushing it deeper still.

Carlin vomits and cries out. Not for mercy, but for death.

In the storm, no one hears.

SEVEN

Lights from a state police cruiser cut the night and spin through the rain. Parked alongside it are a couple state vehicles, a pickup and a SUV. Greer rolls to a stop and tries to get a better look at the situation. The road ahead is flooded out, and the state workers are hurrying about, rushing through the rain in an attempt to construct a temporary blockade outfitted with yellow emergency lights. A lone state policeman in a rain slicker, his hat wrapped in plastic, stands in the middle of the road motioning for her to stop.

Greer pulls up beside him and drops her window a bit. Rain sprays in. "What's happening, officer?"

"Evening, ma'am. We're closing the road due to flooding."

She cranes her neck; sees water gushing across the road beyond the blockade, and what appears to be a small section of cracked pavement that has lifted up and away from the rest of the road. "Great, now what?"

"I'm going to have to ask you to turn your vehicle around and head back in the direction you came."

"Is there another route I can take? I'm headed out of state obviously."

A heavy burst of wind slams a sheet of rain down on them. The cop turns away to absorb the impact. "Yes," he says, facing her again, "but odds are the snow will be here by the time you've finished hooking all the way around. Got a mess out here tonight—flash floods everywhere, several washed out roads—and it's getting worse. Within the hour even most police and emergency vehicles are going to be called in. Terrible storm coming up right behind this one, blizzard conditions expected. My advice is to hunker down for the night, ride this out until morning then see what kind of shape things are in at that point." He leans closer, points to the darkness behind her. "The Moonlight Road Motor Inn's about five miles back. I'm sure they've got vacancies, always do."

Greer nods, she noticed it on her way by. "All right," she says through a heavy sigh. "Thank you, officer."

"Drive safely, ma'am."

She forces a smile, raises the window and makes a slow U-turn, watching the scene grow smaller in her rearview as she starts back. *Poor guy*, she thinks, *he's earning his money out there tonight.*

Headlights pass her in the other direction, heading right for the roadblock. They are the first signs of life Greer has seen on the highway in a long while. *You'll be turning around sooner than you think.* As the taillights vanish in the night she considers the policeman's suggestion. The idea of stopping at some roadside motel is far from appealing, but maybe the cop's right, it's probably better, not to mention safer, to just ride out the storm. *Besides*, she thinks, *I've been driving for hours and I'm exhausted. Be nice to get out of these shoes.*

At the very edge of her headlight beams something separates from the darkness and moves into her line of vision. As if stepping directly out of the night itself, it turns to face her, arms outstretched in welcome.

"Jesus!" Greer slams the brakes and her eyes lock on those of a man in the middle of the road. The same man she saw walking earlier, in the duster.

As the Audi fishtails she cuts the wheel to prevent a sideways skid. Tires screeching and the world spinning past at dizzying speeds, it isn't until she's lurched to a complete stop that she sees another set of headlights bearing down on her, followed by a second screech of tires as the driver slams his brakes and skids toward her through the rain.

Greer grips the wheel tight, closes her eyes and waits for the horrific sound of impact.

It never comes.

She opens her eyes. The other car has stopped within a few feet of the Audi, the lights pouring into her car and making it impossible for her to make out much else. After a moment the car reverses then pulls over onto the side of the road. Heart pounding, Greer does the same.

Did I hit the man in the road? Christ, I must have, he was right—

A sudden pounding on her window startles her back to the present. She looks up, sees a young man in a long raincoat and black knit hat standing next to her car—evidently the driver of the second vehicle—talking to her, but between the glass and the pouring rain, Greer can't make out a word he says. He doesn't appear angry, more concerned and confused.

She lowers the window a little and says, "I'm so sorry, are you OK?"

"Yeah," the man says. "Are you?"

"I think so, yes. I…"

"I was behind you. Why did you slam your brakes on like that?"

Trembling, she wipes at the corners of her mouth with her thumb and index finger. "There was a man, a—

"I almost ran right into you."

"A man in the road—I—I think I hit him."

"A man?" he asks as if he no longer understands the language Greer's speaking. "In the road?"

"Yes, he—he walked right out in front of me. Didn't you see him?"

The man turns and looks out at the highway. He takes a few steps away from the car then comes back. "There's no one there, lady."

"I'm telling you, I saw a man, I—he—there was a man in the road."

He moves around to the front of her car, inspects it then returns. "Lady, there's no damage to your car at all. Trust me, if you hit somebody you'd have all sorts of frontend damage. There's nothing, not even a scratch."

"OK, all right, fine." She waves at him dismissively.

The man stares at her. There is something hard about him, tough, and yet he seems genuinely concerned. He glances at a set of headlights moving through the darkness from the direction they're both headed then looks back at her. "You sure you're all right?"

Greer nods. "I'm just tired, I—with the storm and all, I—again, I'm sorry."

"Hey, no harm no foul." He shrugs and smiles. "Dark stormy night like this, mind can play all kinds of tricks on you. Be careful. Have a good night."

Greer shields her eyes from the oncoming headlights. *He should flag that car down,* she thinks, *tell him not to bother and that he might as well turn around now.* "You too. Thanks."

She closes the window and offers a final smile, but as the lights pass the man is suddenly gone, swept away into the night in the blink of an eye.

More screeching tires, and she looks to her rearview, squinting in an attempt to see through the rain.

A white van has stopped several feet behind her in the middle of the road. It slowly begins to circle back.

Lying in the road between her position and the van is the man in the raincoat and knit hat, facedown, half his body in the breakdown lane, the other half in the road.

"Oh my God!" Greer opens the door and nearly falls out onto the pavement. Scrambling back to her feet, she slips her way to the rear of the Audi and leans against it. The man is not moving. "Oh—Oh my God!"

The van that struck him rolls slowly toward them.

Greer runs to the man, crouches down and touches the center of his back. He's breathing. "Can you hear me?" she calls out above the din of the storm.

"Bastard hit me," he moans, barely conscious.

"Stay still and try not to move, OK? I'll get help, there's— it'll be all right, help's on the way."

She stands, waves at the van to hurry. But it just keeps creeping slowly towards them, headlights illuminating the rain, which has now become an icy slush. *The hell with this ass,* she thinks. She runs back to her car, leans in and snatches her cell from the passenger seat.

The van comes to a stop in the middle of the road. A man steps out.

Greer's mouth falls open, but nothing comes out. No scream. Nothing. She can't even exhale. The same man in the duster she's seen all night—at the burning car and in the road just now—stands in the rain not ten feet from her, an enormous knife in his hand.

Before she can fully comprehend what's taken place, the man is standing right next to her. The rain pools and drips from his hat, his eyes concealed in shadows and night. He reaches out, takes the phone from her hand and crushes it effortlessly, like one might crumple a scrap of paper. Greer stands paralyzed in terror as he opens his palm then leans in and blows as if to disperse ash from his hand. The pieces of phone fly away with the wind as he slowly brings his other hand closer, running the tip of the knife blade up toward Greer's throat.

"Who are you?" she manages, gasping for air.

He cocks his head slightly but says nothing.

"What do you want?"

The man leans close, as if to sniff her, and then answers in a quiet but gravelly, inhuman voice. *"Everything inside you."*

"Motherfucker," someone says over the man's shoulder, the speech slurred and weak, barely audible above the wind and rain. "Mother*fucker*!"

The man in the raincoat and knit hat struggles to all fours, but when he tries to stand he topples back over onto his back and lies still on the side of the road like an overturned turtle.

The knife brings Greer back to the monstrosity before her. Although the pressure of it against the base of her throat is horrifying, she will not simply stand there and let this man kill her. She will fight with everything she has to—

Suddenly the man steps back, spooked. He looks to the road over her shoulder and a low growl similar to that of a feline emanates from deep in his throat. With a sneer he leaves her. The duster billows in the wind and kicks up the smell of death as he returns to the van and drives off in the direction of the blockade.

Shaking uncontrollably, Greer looks back over her shoulder. Headlights leading the way, a small vintage-style car pulls over on the other side of the road. An older man in a black suit emerges. Without saying a word, and seemingly oblivious to the rain, he crosses the street, quickly checks over the man in the raincoat, then helps him up into a sitting position. The man is clearly dazed and a bit bloodied but doesn't appear to be as severely injured as Greer initially suspected. The man in the suit helps him to his feet and back across the street to his car. Once he has him in the passenger seat he walks back over Greer, his face expressionless. "Do you want to live?"

Greer wipes rain from her eyes, certain she's lost her mind. "Wha-what?"

"*Do you want to live?*"

"Yes."

"Then listen very carefully to me and do exactly as I say. If we stay out here in the open we'll die. There's a motel just up the road. It's not ideal but it's all we've got, so that's where we need to be. Get in your car and follow me. Do it now."

"That man, he—"

He turns on his heels and strides back across the lanes to his car.

Shivering and soaked, Greer hurries through the rain to the Audi as the Bel Air whips around and accelerates into the night.

EIGHT

There, in the freezing downfall, the lighted sign of the Moonlight Road Motor Inn cuts the thick rain. Behind it, in the office, dim lights burn. The front desk is unmanned. Adjacent to the main building, the units sit dark, surreal and dreamlike, a mirage amidst miles of empty highway and night without end.

Greer pulls in alongside the Bel Air. Still trembling, she gets out and watches the road for signs of the van. The man in the suit gets out of the Bel Air, moves around to the other side and helps the man in the raincoat from his seat. Though bruised and hobbled with a bit of a limp, he looks to be all right.

"Did you call for help?" she asks frantically.

"I don't have a cell."

"You don't—who doesn't have a cell in this day and age?"

He glares at her with the bluest eyes she's ever seen.

Greer halfheartedly points at the man in the raincoat. "Are you all right?"

"The van just clipped me," he says. "Got lucky."

"Do you have a phone? We need to call the police."

He shakes his head. "It's back in my car."

"Well there must be one in the motel."

"Phones and his car are the least of our worries," the older man says, propping the man in the raincoat against the side of the car. "Trust me."

"That man almost killed us. We need to call for help right now."

"He was here, which means the phone lines have already been cut."

"How do you know he was here?"

He points to the glass front door to the office. "That's his mark."

Greer looks to the door. An inverted cross perhaps a foot long, inside a circle and with what appears to be hastily-drawn depictions of a small heart, club, spade and diamond decorating either side of it has been painted on the glass about halfway down the door. "Is that *blood*?"

"What else would it be?" He moves around to the trunk and pops it. "Right now we've got more important things to focus on than getting to a phone. We'll be lucky if we live the night."

"*What* is going on?" Greer wanders closer to the office. When he offers no response she says, "He won't get far headed in the direction he took off in. The road's flooded, washed out. He's headed straight for a roadblock."

"That means he'll be turning around and coming back this way just like we did," the man in the raincoat says.

"But there's a policeman there," Greer reminds him, "and a couple state workers, they—"

"For their sake I hope they're gone by the time he gets there." The older man removes a large nylon bag from the trunk. "If not, they're already dead."

"Then let's drive back the way we came until we find help or a—"

"I just came from that direction. Heavy snow's falling back there and it's coming this way fast. We're trapped." He gazes out at the road, almost lovingly. "And so is he."

"Who is he?"

"The Devil. And now he knows your name." He looks at Greer, as if for the first time. "We need to move. Enough questions."

"Oh, well excuse me if I'm not accustomed to—"

"Well you better get accustomed to it." The man walks past her toward the office. "Now move your ass or that's all they'll find out here come morning."

Taken aback but still too confused and frightened to argue with him, Greer cautiously approaches the man in the raincoat. "Are you OK to walk?"

"Yeah," he says, "just a little banged up."

"Did he tell you anything?"

"I don't know any more than you do, lady."

"Greer," she says, offering her hand.

"Luke." He accepts it. "You're shaking."

"I'm scared to death."

"Can't blame you on that one." He releases her hand and pushes away from the car with a muffled grunt. "Not sure I like the look of this place. Maybe you're right and we should take our chances on the road."

"Not with a blizzard coming in. All those miles of isolated highway, it'd be suicide. We'd die out there."

The older man stops at the office door, drops the nylon bag then reaches into his jacket pocket and removes a small suede pouch with a drawstring. He mumbles something the others can't hear then reaches into the pouch and tosses a handful of what appears to be salt against the mark on the door. Despite the rain the blood drawing remains intact due to an overhanging ledge above the door, so the man reaches out, and using his forearm, smudges it until it's nothing more than a swath of blood on glass.

Greer hugs herself in the cold rain. "What the hell is he doing?"

"No clue."

Bells over the door to the office jingle above the rain. They watch the man slip inside. "He just came out of nowhere."

"So did the other guy," Luke says.

"And for some reason, him showing up when he did saved us back there." Greer shivers, tries to dislodge memories of the nightmare in the duster pressing the knife against her throat. "Obviously he knows a lot more about what's going on than he's telling us."

"Let's get out of this rain and find out what we can."

Together, they walk to the office.

At least it's warmer and dry inside, but as they enter it's clear something terrible has happened here, something violent. Several sheets of paper covered in text, many marked up with red pen, lay scattered across the floor, and what's left of a laptop is in pieces behind the front desk. A knapsack lies on a small couch just inside the front door, contents emptied onto the cushions and floor.

The door to the office behind the front desk is open and hanging on a single hinge, torn free of the other, and a small worn army jacket hangs on the back of the desk chair inside the office, but there are no signs of its owner or any employees for that matter. A small adjacent bathroom is also empty.

Luke leans against the front desk, still favoring his leg. "What's going on?" he asks the man in the black suit. "What was that you threw against the door?"

"Salt." He moves to the couch, drops the nylon bag there and unzips it. "It's a purification ritual."

Greer and Luke exchange troubled glances.

"A purification ritual," Greer says. "What are you purifying?"

"Evil." The man reaches into the bag, comes back with a pump shotgun and a box of shells. "Do either of you know how to handle firearms?"

By the time the man looks back at them Luke is already holding his gun, a .38 snub-nose revolver. Though down by his leg, it's obvious he's comfortable with it and schooled in its use. "You saved our asses back there, dog, and I appreciate it. But who the hell walks around with the kind of firepower you got in that bag? I don't know you. Don't know anything about you. So I'm gonna need some answers on what's going on here, or we got a problem."

Unimpressed, the man loads the shotgun. "What are your names?"

He hesitates a moment then says, "I'm Luke. This is Greer, what's—"

"Doc Banta. OK? Now we're all formerly introduced." He motions to Luke. "For the sake of brevity I'll assume you're not just a poser and can actually handle a piece. Good." He glances at Greer. "What about you?"

"Me? I've never fired a gun in my life."

Doc nods though he's clearly disappointed. "More than likely going to be a skill you'll need to acquire as soon as possible."

"Look, man," Luke says, "who the hell are you? And why did that maniac out there try to kill us?"

"He hunts humans. I hunt him."

"OK, so he's some sort of deranged serial killer? And you're what? A cop or a bounty hunter or some shit?"

"I wish that's all he was. He's been killing for longer than you can even imagine. Unless we stop him he'll keep coming until we're all dead." Doc racks the shotgun. "And no, I'm not a cop. He murdered my family. I've been tracking him for years."

"*Years?*"

"It's all come down to this. One way or another this ends tonight."

Greer brings her hands to her head. "This cannot be happening."

"He's already been here," Doc tells them, "which means everyone else that was here is now dead. I found the register on the floor there behind the desk. According to the sign-ins there are two parties staying here, a single and a couple. We need to find them. I'm warning you both right now, they won't be alive, but I need to know what he's done. I'll explain more when we have time. But for now you're just going to have to trust me. We need to do a quick check of the premises, and we need to keep watch too. How's your leg, Luke?"

"I'll live."

Doc points to a fuse box on the wall behind the front desk. "The road sign is sure to be on one of those toggles. Find it. Then watch the road. Anything or anybody comes anywhere near this place, throw the switch, kill the sign and then turn it back on. That'll be the signal. Got it?"

Wearily, Luke nods.

"Greer is it?"

"Yes, Greer Fields."

"You come with me."

She glances at Luke then looks back at Doc and smiles nervously, involuntarily. "Listen, I'm in *sales*, OK?"

"I know you're scared," he tells her. "But please do as I say. We don't have a lot of time, and it's our only chance."

Greer looks deep into Doc's icy blue eyes. She sees many things. Honor is among them. "All right," she says softly.

"Here it comes." Luke points at the parking lot.

Outside, the rain has turned to snow.

NINE

He closes his eyes, sees the bodies fall. One after the next, in sprays of blood, they topple and collapse. Mountains of nude mutilated corpses surround him amidst fires burning in rusted trashcans, in the windows of gutted, long abandoned buildings, in the derelict, rotted carcasses of cars. A city of death and disease, a beautiful memory of what once was and will be again. The world is on fire when he dreams, when he is quiet. When he contemplates.

And then the road. Always the road. Waiting. It's never far. Stretched out before him for miles. It is his altar. Those he finds there, his sacrifices. Dark or light, it makes no difference. There is death there, unimaginable violence. It beckons him, seduces him, hiding on those lonely roads and endless highways.

Cursed to wander, he can neither look away nor refuse. It is his destiny. His life. His death. His prison. His escape. But he will not fade away. When it's his time he will cross in a brilliant bloodbath of horror and tears, the screams of those he's slaughtered his chorus as he passes to nirvana, bringing with him the tortured souls he has worked so hard to horde.

Home, he thinks. *It's been so long...so very long...but soon now. Soon.*

He remembers jeweled elephants passing through clouds of incense, and the sparkling robes of Rajas of India... the beautifully deadly songs of great Zulu warriors beating their shields in Africa... the echoes of sacrificial prayers in stone temples of South America... the ethereal chants in monasteries of Nepal... the rumbling music of Aborigines playing didgeridoos in the wilds of Australia... the tribal dances and percussive sounds of Native Americans... the ring-forts of the ancient Celts in Europe, their women in embroidered dresses, hair in intricate braids, the men boldly clad in animal skins and cloaks... the sands of ancient Arabia, the nomads, the holy cities of Mecca and Medina... the power, violence and decadence of the Roman Empire...the pyramids, the Great Sphinx of Giza and all the pageantry, mysticism and mysteries of Egypt... he remembers it all.

And he weeps with his memories, weeps until the darkness returns and reminds him who he is, what he is, bringing with it the power, the evil, the rage. Death. It is incomprehensibly freeing to kill others when one cannot die oneself, because everything that lives needs death as much as it needs life. It is the way of things, the natural course. But then, he is not natural. He is a deviant, an aberration. He is only normal in the flames, in the blood, the horror. There, he is home, and there, with his collected souls, he will find peace and perhaps even joy, if he can ever know such a thing. Can Evil ever truly know joy, *real* joy? He cannot be sure. Even with centuries to ponder such questions, some answers continue to elude him.

"The things I've seen," he whispers to the night. "The roads I've traveled."

But he is tired.

Over the years he has attempted to explain such things to his sacrifices, but they never understand. They accuse him of being insane—which of course he is—but that's hardly the point.

Perhaps this will be his swansong, his masterpiece. Perhaps he will finally be set free and his work here will be done, the curse lifted. Tonight. This night.

The one hunting him is close. He can smell him.

The others, he can smell them too.

None of them realize how much they need him; how the darkness in each of them brought him to them, and how he will eventually do what is necessary to set them all free.

He looks up at the falling snow. *It's almost as beautiful as flame*, he thinks, *and just as deadly.*

Watching the snowfall, he leans against the side of the van, takes the deck of cards from his pocket and absently shuffles them with one hand. Later, he will play the game. Once all this is over. Then, and not a moment before, it will be time.

There are rules, rituals that must be followed.

He returns the deck to his pocket, wipes some snow from his face, and gazes at the highway. He glances down at his hand. It's covered in blood. He raises it to his face a second time and wipes more away. The last one bled like a pig. It sprayed his face and until then he'd forgotten.

Smiling at his carelessness, he takes a bandana from his duster pocket, thoroughly wipes his face clean then opens the rear doors of the van.

Just inside the otherwise cluttered interior is his knapsack. Next to it in a pool of blood and a tangle of tendons and gore is Carlin's head, the eyes still open and staring into eternity, the mouth frozen in the twisted grimace it wore at the moment of death. He reaches out and tenderly, lovingly strokes one cheek and then the other.

After a moment he opens the knapsack and rummages around until he finds what he needs, a small scalpel, surgical scissors and a thick needle roughly the size of a standard pencil. He puts the items on the floor of the van, quickly looks through his personal things then turns to the other weapons in the knapsack, a crossbow, a shotgun and two handguns. The black crossbow is outfitted with a scope, is whisper-quiet and launches arrows at three hundred and seventy-five feet per second. The arrows are razor-tipped and designed for maximum penetration of large game. Next to it is a Mossberg six-shot pump shotgun with a pistol grip, a ten-round 9mm Glock, and a six-shot Smith & Wesson .357 Magnum, along with numerous boxes of ammunition. Although he cares for each weapon meticulously, he carefully and thoroughly inspects each one then returns them to the knapsack.

Next, he retrieves the scalpel, and while holding Carlin's head tight to the van bed with his free hand, carves the eyes out with a horrible wet sound he has grown used to. Once the eyeballs have been removed from the sockets he snips the cords with the scissors to completely free them from the head then returns the tools to the knapsack. He zips it shut, places it on the ground next to the van then takes the eyeballs and wipes them clean with the bandana.

Now they are ready.

He removes his hat, places it on Carlin's head then opens wide his duster. He removes a leather cord from around his neck and looks at it fondly. Hanging from it are what at first glance appear to be pieces of dried and darkened fruit of some kind, but closer inspection reveals human eyeballs strung together to form a necklace. He threads the large needle with one end of the necklace and then punctures his newest additions, pulls the needle through and adds them to the collection. Once finished he slides the needle into his coat pocket then proudly slips the necklace over his head.

After a quiet prayer to the dark, he takes his hat back, puts it on then palms Carlin's head and tosses it away over his shoulder. *God is good.*

As the head bounces along the breakdown lane, he decides he'll walk. Nice night for a slow walk in the snow, and it will give him time to prepare, to think, to manage the fires in his mind.

The van is on the side of the road and his knapsack easily within reach. He unscrews and tosses away the plastic gas cap then stuffs the bandana in the tank, leaving a small portion hanging out and flopping in the wind. He removes a box of stick matches from his coat, strikes one, cups it and lights up the bandana.

Several feet in front of the van a roadblock has been setup. Little yellow lights blink through the snow and darkness. He'd like to smash them to pieces, but there seems little point, so instead he hoists his knapsack onto his shoulder and heads off on foot in the direction of the motel.

Burn.

A moment later, the van explodes in a burst of flames that light up the night with a magnificent flash. He does not look back, but he can feel the rush of heat and smell the gasoline and smoke.

In time, there is only the road.

And like all the others in every corner of his world, those weary lambs that wait for him along the way.

TEN

Just as Doc predicted, the phone at the front desk has been torn from the wall and the extension in the office has been ripped free as well. Luke holds one of the useless phones in his hand a moment then throws it aside with disgust.

Greer quickly rummages through her Gucci handbag until she finds a colored rubber hairband. Tossing the purse on the front desk, she pulls her tawny hair back into a short ponytail and secures it with the band. She has seen the way Luke looks at her, like she's some spoiled bitch, with her expensive car, designer jeans, Ferragamo flats, wool cardigan jacket and Christian Bernard watch. Funny how if a man looks successful he's respected and seen as a go-getter, but let a woman have the same look and most men immediately assume she's some sugar daddy's toy or got it through sordid means. What never occurs to those types is that she probably earned it just like anyone else. Doc, on the other hand, is clearly laser-focused and barely seems to notice her with any sort of depth whatsoever. She's spent her professional life assessing clients, reading people and making her moves based on those assessments. And her skills in that area have served her well. The younger guy is easier to read—as younger people usually are—but she hasn't been around him long enough to be sure if his act is genuine or not. Is he a wannabe tough guy or the real deal? Looks hardened, like a criminal type, but that may be presumptuous at this point. The older one, Doc, he's more of an enigma. There's a lot going on there, and a lot of it's frightening. He's a slow boil type, the kind who's been raging inside for a very long time and could blow at any moment. Greer doesn't trust either of them, but what choice does she have? She looks to Doc, gives him a quick nod.

Behind the front desk Luke finds the breaker for the sign. "How much time do we have?"

"Probably not enough," Doc answers. "Let's move."

Greer joins him, and together, they head out into the storm.

Luke limps over to the front of the office and stands before the glass front wall so he can have a clear view of the lot, the units to his left and the highway in both directions. Snow is already beginning to accumulate, blowing across the road and spattering the motel walls. He watches Doc and Greer hurry along to the dirt lot and the awaiting units then looks back over his shoulder at the Gucci handbag on the counter. Normally he'd have already gone through it. Probably some cash, plenty of credit cards, a decent little score. But now, all he can think about is Rachel. *God, get me through this*, he prays, *and I'll go home, I'll change. I'll get her back and be a better man. You'll see. Just give me one more chance.* He fingers the gun in his coat pocket. He's never shot anyone, but if it comes down to it he will. At least he assures himself of this.

Fuck comes anywhere near me again and I'll put a bullet in his head.

Sounds so good he almost believes it. But the fear reminds him he's vulnerable—they all are—and he realizes then just how quiet it is here. He looks to Doc's gun bag. If need be he's got additional firepower. The papers scattered across the floor and the knapsack on the couch distracts him. Who did they belong to? He wonders. A plethora of visions flood his mind, offering various versions of what might've happened, but he flushes them away and focuses again on the highway.

He's out there somewhere, not so very far away. And he's coming.

The Devil, Doc called him.

He reaches under his shirt and grips the silver crucifix hanging from his neck. He's found comfort in it ever since he's been a little boy. His mother gave it to him and growing up he spent many nights clutching it and asking God for help, for rescue. When it didn't arrive he pleaded for silence, for the sounds of his drunken father beating his crying mother to go away. Instead, he learned how to be quiet himself, to pull the covers up tight over his head and to close his eyes tight as he could. He learned to hide in the silence.

Luke blinks away the memories and the tears that normally accompany them. Rubs the crucifix. Watches the road.

And doesn't make a sound.

The wind comes in harsh, freezing spurts. Doc leads the way as he and Greer cross the lot and close on the long row of dark units. The snow, heavy, wet and falling fast, reminds them that the night is alive, and that while the property is eerily quiet and the highway is a dark and deserted expanse of shadows and swirling powder, they are not alone.

Two lonely vehicles sit parked and dark, slowly disappearing as little by little the snow covers them. Doc remembers the sign-in log: a single in Unit 14 and a double in Unit 10. He and Greer leave the dirt lot for a narrow strip of cement that runs the length of the units, and after passing the first nine doors, come to a stop.

Doc looks back at her, his long silver hair blowing in the wind. "You don't want to see what's in there," he tells her. "Stay out here, keep your eyes open and watch my back. You see anything, start screaming."

Greer nods but says nothing, shaking from the cold, fear, or both.

He slowly turns the knob for Unit 10. The door opens, as he knew it would. Steeling himself for what he is about to find, he pushes it open.

The room is dark. Holding the shotgun with one hand, he reaches in with the other and feels around until he locates a wall switch just to the right of the door. He flips it.

Even before he steps inside he can see the carnage. Like all the times before, he tries not to look at first, but even in peripheral vision it is too horrific to ignore. He moves deeper into the room, lowers the shotgun and covers his nose and mouth with his forearm. The stench is unbearable.

The walls are covered with The Dealer's handiwork, his ciphers and spells painted in blood and bodily fluids from one end of the room to the other. On the floor not five feet from where Doc stands are a pair of dismembered human legs. Bare and spattered with blood, they look like pieces from a mannequin lying there on the carpet. Until he looks closer and sees the painted toenails, the softness of the flesh, the gold ankle bracelet and the small four-leaf clover tattoo on the side of one calf. The rest of the young woman has been left on the bed, face-up, the arms removed as well and nailed to the wall above the bed to form a cross. Her eyes are gone, and her abdomen and vaginal region have been severely, brutally mutilated. There is an unlit black ceremonial candle inside her.

Doc guesses she's twenty. Maybe.

He walks through the slaughterhouse, stepping over pieces of human flesh, internal organs and puddles of blood, urine and fecal matter until he reaches the bathroom. The door is open. The tiles are slick with blood, and what was once a young man is hanging upside down from a section of exposed pipe above the shower. His ankles have been bound with rope. He's been skinned from head to toe, a raw, red, bloody wet mess. His ears are in the sink. Above the sink, written in blood, is a prayer in a language Doc cannot read and doesn't understand but has seen The Dealer use before. He leans over the sink for a closer look. Something has been placed between the ears and partially burned. A playing card. The Ace of Hearts.

More rituals. More spells. More evil. More madness. More death.

He's ramping it up, Doc thinks.

He leaves the room, closing the door behind him, glad to be out in the cold and snow again. At least out here the air is fresh and he can breathe. He leans against the building a moment and closes his eyes. Over time, like a hardened combat veteran, he has learned to handle the carnage and atrocities of such scenes. The Dealer leaves nothing but blood and death in his wake, and Doc has been swimming in it for longer than he cares to remember. He never vomits anymore, rarely cries—unless it's a child—and generally manages to keep his wits about him. Just the same, each time he walks through a killing scene, it takes a little bit more from him, damages him just a little bit deeper.

"Are you all right?" Greer asks.

He nods.

"What's in there?"

"You don't want to know."

"No, I don't. But I need to."

He looks at her. She's white as a ghost and looks like she's freezing, but he believes her. She's tougher than he initially thought. "If you go through that door," he warns, "you'll never get what's in there out of your head."

She swallows. Hard. "Then tell me."

"Young couple. Slaughtered. He's on a feeding frenzy like I've never seen before, but there's meaning behind it. There's meaning behind everything he does." Doc pushes away from the wall and starts toward Unit 14. "Come on."

Greer follows. "What do you mean by feeding frenzy?"

"Just keep your eyes open."

They arrive at Unit 14. The door is already ajar. Doc pokes at it with the barrel of the shotgun, pushes it partially open. Again, no light, he always leaves them in darkness. Doc draws a deep breath, paws some snow from his face then steps inside. He finds a switch in the same spot just to the right of the door.

Bathed in light, the room comes to life, but it is not what he expected.

No blood. No body. No mayhem. Just an empty motel room.

He takes it in, quickly, efficiently.

An unopened suitcase in the corner. A set of car keys on the bureau along with a wallet and a cellphone—no—just a cellphone case. The phone is in pieces on the carpet. The bed is made but the comforter is rumpled and bares a vague human outline. Loafers on the floor next to the bed. Balled up black nylon socks inside. A suit jacket over the back of the desk chair on the far wall. A small appointment book on the desk. A raincoat hanging in the open closet.

Doc moves to the bathroom. The door is closed but seeping from the bottom of the door is what appears to be diluted blood.

He opens the door, finds a switch and lights up the room.

The remains of a man float face-up in the bathtub. Still fully clothed, he has been gutted from pubic bone to sternum and the water has turned an odd pinkish shade in some areas and a deep black in others. One of the man's arms dangles over the side of the tub. His hand has been chopped clean off, the wrist a mangled bloody stump.

No other signs or evidence of ritual or magic.

He didn't care much about this one, Doc thinks. *He just got in the way.*

He rejoins Greer outside. She stares intently at something across the lot.

"What is it?" Doc asks.

She shakes her head so subtly he barely notices. "I'm not sure, it's just...what the hell *is* that?"

He follows her gaze. Something moves in the darkness, through the snow. Something perhaps twenty feet above the ground in the middle of the parking lot, gently swaying in the wind.

"Do you see it? There, it's moving with the wind."

"I see it," Doc says. He follows the shape up higher into the sky and notices something else just barely visible in the darkness and snow. He looks to the road. Nothing. Without another word he starts off across the lot with Greer in tow.

Just before they reach the object, Doc steps in something wet and spongy that makes a squishing sound beneath his weight. He springs back and looks down at a human liver wrapped in several feet of intestines tangled about it like slimy lengths of rope. He looks up, realizes now that there is a flagpole in the center of the dirt lot he hadn't before noticed. The snow has not yet managed to fully cover the entrails or the enormous halo of blood staining the ground at the base of the pole. Behind him, Greer gags. No flags fly, but the decapitated body of a heavyset man hangs upside down by his feet, arms dangling low and swinging in the wind.

Before Doc can get her out of there Greer doubles over, vomits, and then staggers back in the direction of the motel.

She stops and turns back to him, wiping her mouth with the back of her hand. "Jesus Christ! Where the fuck is his head?"

"He took it."

"*Why?*"

"Body parts are very important in his black magic." Doc starts toward her. "He's building his power, consolidating it. He knows I'm close, he knows this is it for one of us. Showdown's coming and there's no way out."

"This has nothing to do with me, I—"

"We need to get back inside."

"I don't want to be in the middle of this!"

"It's too late for all that. He's drawn to you, to all of us."

"What the hell are you talking about? He doesn't even know me!"

"He knows you enough. Trust me, he can smell you from miles away. He can see your nightmares while you sleep, hear your darkest thoughts when you're awake. They draw him to you." She looks at him helplessly. He's seen it before in many others but can only hope this time things will end differently. "Greer, we need to get inside. Now. Right now."

"But..." she points to the body without looking at it, "we can't just leave the pour soul up there like that."

"His soul's not here anymore." Pulse pounding in his ears, Doc grips the shotgun tight, takes Greer by the arm and keeps walking, pulling her along behind him as he goes. "It belongs to The Dealer now."

ELEVEN

Body aching, Luke moves back to the front desk and leans against it a moment. He runs a hand over his face. It comes back with flecks of dried blood from the bloody nose he had earlier and a patch of road rash on the right side of his forehead. He can't remember the entire event out on the road but does recall the impact, how he just barely got out of the way before the van clipped him and sent him airborne. Throughout his life Luke has been involved in numerous physical confrontations, and in some cases has endured tremendous beatings at the hands of other men. But never in his life has he been struck by anything with such violence. It is the closest he's ever come to death, and he can still feel the residue of terror and confusion coursing through his veins.

Where is the sonofabitch? Is he really coming back, or has he moved on, barreling down that dark and desolate highway in search of new victims? The tension is unbearable and reminds him of his time in prison when the block would become deathly quiet. Whenever the constant din in prison ceases, it means something's about to go down. Something bad. Something violent. Everyone waits. Quietly. Knowing sooner or later the screams will come, the pleading and begging for mercy, and finally, more silence. And then comes the eruption, the screams of those who have survived and live on in this hell while the victim lies dead or dying nearby. They cling to the bars in their cells and holler like the mad dogs they've become, some in protest, some in fear, some with sadistic joy, all with violence and insanity and release, a human zoo of caged, primal lunacy.

Having watched the road for several minutes through the heavy snow, Luke's eyes burn and sting, but his mind continues to race. How the hell did he end up here, in the middle of this mess? *Just like that last cashier*, he thinks, *wrong place, wrong time.*

He looks around the office, taking it all in with closer attention this time, occasionally glancing back out at the parking lot and highway beyond.

Same as on the floor, several sheets of paper lie scattered across the front desk counter. One in particular catches his eye. It takes a moment to register, but once it does Luke's heart drops. How had he missed this before?

A shoeprint. Stamped onto the piece of paper.

Luke looks up. Drop ceiling.

He listens carefully for any sounds of movement or even breathing.

Nothing.

He follows the section of ceiling directly above the shoeprint to an air vent on the wall alongside the front desk. If a person stood on the counter, removed the vent cover and gripped the bottom of the vent, they might be able to pull themselves up diagonally then climb into the vent.

Luke takes a closer look at the vent cover. Although in place, it's not secured with screws and is instead the style that is hinged and simply swings open with a pull. So had someone fled into the vent they could've easily closed the grate behind them, thereby leaving no trace of their escape.

He stares up at the slots in the vent cover. If someone were hiding in the shaft they'd be able to see him, but he couldn't see them.

The bells over the door sound and Luke whirls around, gun leveled.

Greer stands just inside the door, pale and drawn, hands raised and eyes teeming with panic and fear.

Luke lowers the gun. "Where's Doc?"

"Getting something from his car." She brushes snow from her shoulders and arms but continues shaking, her face a tangled web of emotion and shock. "It's just like he said. They're all dead. One in one room, two in another, and..." Greer hesitates, struggling with what she is about to tell him, as it's still difficult to believe. "Luke, there's a dead body hanging from the flagpole. Decapitated."

Luke's response is barely audible. "Jesus."

Greer hugs herself. "It's a goddamn bloodbath out there and he—that man he—he had a knife right to my throat, the same knife he probably used to—"

"Take it easy."

"Take it easy? *Take is easy*? You fucking take it easy!"

This time it's Luke who holds his hands up. "I didn't mean anything by it, all right? Just stay calm, try not to freak. You don't want to lose it. Not here. Not now. You go off that edge, you might not make it back. You feel me?"

He's right, and she knows it. Greer nods and does her best to release some of the tension in her body.

Before Luke can say anything else the door opens again, and Doc enters along with a burst of snow and cold wind. He carries a small black leather bag. "You're supposed to be watching the road."

"I am, I—"

"Stay on it." Doc leans his shotgun against the front desk, places the bag on the counter and begins rummaging through it. "He's close, I can feel him."

"Something you need to look at." Once he has Doc's attention, Luke taps a finger on the sheet of paper marked with the shoeprint then subtly cocks his head in the direction of the vent.

Doc responds with an equally subtle nod. He thought he'd accounted for all the vehicles parked outside, but if the van The Dealer was driving came from here as well then the little Honda out front belongs to someone else. Due to where it's parked, he assumes it's another employee, someone who was manning the front desk when The Dealer arrived. From the small size of the print it is most likely a woman, and if she's escaped up into the vent shaft, has survived and is still hiding somewhere in the ductwork, she poses no immediate threat.

"Watch the road," he says evenly. "I have to secure this place best I can then we'll deal with that."

"He tries coming through that door he won't make it." Luke holds the .38 up for effect. "Between the two of us he can't—"

"That might slow him down. It won't stop him."

"I put one in his head it'll stop him."

"No. It won't."

"He ain't Superman, bro."

"I already told you what he is."

"I'm not scared of the Devil."

"Well you should be."

In a misguided battle of wills, they hold each other's stares for several seconds. Luke breaks first, looking away before limping back over to the front of the office to resume his guard duty.

Unsure of what to do, Greer wanders about between them.

Doc removes several items from the leather bag, including a squat white candle, a container of black pepper, a jar containing cloves of garlic, a small wooden bowl, and two small plastic bottles, one filled with water, the other with olive oil. He first takes a pinch of pepper and sprinkles it at the inside threshold of the front door.

"Beware those outside the light who break this bond or attempt to cross this threshold," he mutters. "You will find neither welcome nor refuge here and are forbidden entrance."

Luke and Greer exchange their second troubled glances of the evening.

"What is this?" Luke asks. "More of your voodoo bullshit?"

"Witchcraft," Greer says. "I think."

"Are you fucking kidding me?"

Doc quickly returns to the counter. "Watch the road."

"I been watching the motherfucking road," Luke snaps. "Only thing out there's some snow and ice. I think your boy's long gone."

"He's closer than you realize."

"All I see is you acting a fool and throwing shit on the floor."

Doc mixes water and oil together in the bowl. "You have no idea what you're dealing with or what he's capable of."

"I know no matter how crazy he is he's still a man just like anybody else."

"He *is* crazy, you're right about that. He's completely, hopelessly insane." Doc lights the white candle. "But he's not a man."

"Yeah? Well I don't believe in that mumbo-jumbo, supernatural bullshit."

Doc opens the jar of garlic cloves. "Says the man wearing a crucifix."

"That's right, I believe in Jesus. You don't like it? Fuck you."

"I don't give a rat's ass what you believe." Doc places nine cloves of garlic on the counter. "I'm just trying to keep him out. These purification and protection spells will accomplish that. They won't work indefinitely, his magic is far more powerful than mine, but they'll make do for now."

"Dude got a bag full of guns and he's playing with spells and candles. Fuck you think this is?" Luke looks to Greer for support, but she shrugs and turns away. "All right, fine. Whatever."

One at a time, Doc holds the cloves over the flame. The moment they ignite he drops them into the bowl, one after the next. As they're extinguished a scented smoke is released. He holds the bowl higher, allowing the smoke to crawl higher and across the office area. "Evil, I repel you and purify this space."

After several seconds, Doc goes to the door, opens it and pours the contents of the bowl onto the ground. He then returns the items to the bag, takes up the shotgun and looks up at the vent.

"What?" Greer asks.

Luke leans close, tells her about the shoeprint and whispers, "Think there might be someone up there, maybe another employee that got away, hid up in the vent."

Doc searches the items scattered on the couch from the knapsack until he finds a canvas wallet. He opens it, locates a driver's license. "Kit Piper?" he calls out, walking back toward the vent. "Kit, if you're up there it's all right, we're not going to hurt you. If you can hear me you need to come down from there."

"Kit," Greer chimes in, thinking perhaps another female voice might comfort her, "it's all right, just let us know if you're there, OK?"

"We have to find out if she's up there," Doc says. "It's a vent, which means it leads to a way out."

"And another way in," Luke says.

"Exactly. Odds are it comes out somewhere on the roof. And if she's used it and left an opening up there, he'll find it."

"So throw some mayonnaise up in that bitch and say some more of your heebie-jeebie bullshit," Luke cracks. "We'll be all set."

"If she is up there I'm sure she's scared out of her mind," Greer says. "There's no telling what she saw."

"We've got two options," Doc says.

"We're listening."

"We either check out the vent or we check out the roof. May end up having to do both."

"If she's out in that storm she won't last long," Luke says.

"But if she made it that far why not try to make it to her car?" Greer asks.

Doc moves into the office behind the front desk. The army jacket over the back of the chair is far too small to have belonged to the man on the flagpole. He checks the pockets, comes back with a ring of keys. He returns to the lobby and tosses them on the counter. "Because when she made a break for it she didn't have time to get to her keys."

"So now what?"

"You want to go up there and check it out?" Doc asks Greer.

"Me?"

"You're the only one that'll fit."

"Shit." She rubs her eyes, hoping to dissipate the slight headache lingering there. "Yeah, I—OK—fine." She moves behind the counter.

"It's a relatively short distance to the roof so you're probably only talking about fifty feet or so of shaft system. Once you can see to the end of it, if there's still no sign of her then come back down and I'll go out and check the roof."

"Hold up," Luke says suddenly. "We got a bigger problem."

Doc and Greer turn in unison, drawn to the same thing Luke has seen.

Barely visible in the darkness and heavy snowfall is the silhouette of a man standing in the middle of the road, his duster flapping in the wind.

"Oh my God," Greer whispers.

Something suddenly ignites and encircles him, leaving him in the center of a small ring of fire, the flames reaching nearly halfway up his body and casting him in an eerie golden hue.

Even as the snow slowly begins to extinguish the fire, he extends his arms out on either side of him, throws back his head and begins to laugh.

TWELVE

T hey watch as the last of the flames die and The Dealer is returned to darkness.

"He wants us to know he's here," Doc explains. "He's trying to frighten us."

"It's working," Greer says.

The silhouette backs away, swallowed first by snow, then by night.

Luke starts toward the door, .38 raised.

Doc stops him, grabbing him by the shoulder firmly enough to prevent him from easily taking another step, but with a sufficient amount of restraint so that it isn't perceived as assaultive. "You don't want to go out there, son."

"He's right in the middle of the road. I say we take him down now. He can't stop us both if we hit him at the same time."

"You go out there now it's suicide."

"None of this lighting shit on fire and magic man bullshit means dick to me, all right?" Luke squares his stance. "You want me to keep listening to you, then you better start making some goddamn sense."

"Listen to me or don't, your decision." Doc releases Luke's shoulder and motions to the door. "You want to go out there and try to take him out, go. You'll be dead before you can get a shot off."

"Then what's the plan?"

"We hold our ground."

Luke considers this a moment. "Let him come to us?"

"He will in time. Just not right away, not now. He won't cross this threshold—he can't, not yet—and the emergency door off the office is locked with a heavy-duty bolt and a bar, I already checked it. If he tries to come through that we'll know it. Those are the only ways in, except for the vent, and in his current state he can't fit in it any better than I can."

"His current state?" Greer asks. "What does that mean?"

"Means he's a shape-shifter too," Luke chuckles. "This dude's seen too many horror movies. Where the hell are all the plows and sanders? That's what I want to know."

"The cop at the roadblock told me all emergency vehicles and plows were being called in due to the severity of the storm," Greer says.

"But there's usually sanders and plows out early on trying to stay ahead of this shit."

"Maybe the storm was too fast-moving. The State can't risk stranding a bunch of plows out in the middle of nowhere. By now they've probably either been called in to wait out the storm or they've been moved to roadways closer to higher populated areas. I mean, I don't know for sure but that'd be my guess."

"No one's coming to save us," Doc tells them. "It's just us out here. Us and him, and the sooner you come to terms with that the better off we'll all be."

"Doesn't feel like we're ever gonna be better off again," Luke scoffs.

"The night's young," Doc reminds him. "We have a chance."

"But not a good one."

"No, not a good one."

"I go out, I'm doing it swinging."

I hope so, Doc thinks. "We need to kill the lights in here."

Greer blanches. "Why would we do that?"

"Because with all this glass we can see him," Doc explains. "But with the lights on in here he can see us too. He can see every move we make. Leave the candle burning, it'll provide just enough light for us to get around, but it'll limit what can be seen from outside."

Luke finds the appropriate breakers and throws the first, which kills the road sign. The second plunges the office into near darkness.

"So the only relatively safe way to check the roof with him out there is if I go up through the shaft." Greer eyes the vent again. "But how do we know he won't already be up there by the time I get deep into the shaft?"

Doc watches her through the candlelight. "We don't."

"So you won't let me go out right at this guy with a gun, but she can risk her ass sliding around in a vent shaft looking for somebody who might be on the roof?" Luke shakes his head. "You don't have to go up there."

"I know," Greer says, "but if she's up there or in the shaft somewhere—"

"If she was in the shaft she would've heard us calling her name and she would've answered. She didn't. That only leaves so many options, right? She's either up on the roof or she's not. If she is she's been out there a while now and who knows what kind of shape she's in? If she's not that means she either made a break for it on foot and took her chances in the storm, or she's hiding in one of the units somewhere else in the motel. She could be dead too. Why risk it?"

"Because if she's still alive and hiding up on that roof all alone it's only a matter of time before she freezes to death," Greer responds. "Just like Doc said, no one's coming to save us. If I can get to her and let her know we're here, it might save her life."

"And what if you get up there and she isn't there?"

"I come back down and that's that."

"It's your decision," Doc tells her.

With a heavy sigh, Greer climbs up onto the front desk. "Then let me do this before I change my mind."

Doc goes to his nylon bag and returns with a classic Commando knife in a leather sheath, both of which have been coated with a black finish. "Here," he says, thrusting it at her. "Six-inch stainless-steel blade, razor sharp. Up-close it's about as nasty as they come."

"Comforting." She tentatively accepts it and slides the sheath clip over her belt until it's securely attached.

"Take this too," he adds, handing her his Zippo. "Keep it lit and you'll have no trouble seeing where you're going or what's up ahead of you. If you go all the way to the roof, once you're out there stay low and quiet. There's no way to know where he is out there, but just because you don't see him it doesn't mean he's not close, understand? You get to the roof, do what you can but do it fast."

"I understand."

"We'll stay quiet, you do the same, but if you get into trouble or need help, bang repeatedly on the shaft hard as you can. We'll hear it."

"And do what?"

"Whatever we can."

"Awesome." Greer holds the lighter in her mouth then extends her arms until she's able to reach the grate. With a tug, it swings open. Leaning, she grasps the opening with both hands and pulls herself up, her legs swinging momentarily above the front desk before she's in up to her waist with a stifled grunt. It looks as if she's been spearheaded through the wall, with half of her body embedded and the lower half sticking out. But a second later her legs and feet vanish as she wiggles into the shaft and begins inching her way along on her stomach. As she goes, the shaft echoes and amplifies her every move.

The ventilation shaft is an even tighter squeeze than Greer suspected. She's never been claustrophobic, but the narrow quarters summon a wave of crushing fears nonetheless, particularly as the further she goes the darker it gets. Only a few seconds in, she stops, plucks the lighter from her mouth, breathes awhile then reassures herself she can do this. She flips open the Zippo, ignites it. The flame, higher than she anticipates, nearly reaches the top of the shaft but is quite effective as it easily illuminates an area a foot or two ahead of her.

Christ, she thinks, *looks like some sort of metal tomb.*

Greer continues on, slowly dragging herself through the shaft until she reaches a bend in the road. Once there, she can smell colder, clearer air, but rather than being flat, the shaft proceeds upward at a fairly steep angle. She snaps the Zippo closed. "Just keeps getting better," she mutters, her voice bouncing off the surrounding metal and reverberating all around her.

Bracing with both hands, she hoists herself up and around the turn. As she climbs up the slope she tries to figure out how she came to be here, at this moment, in this place. What she wouldn't give to be back in that last hotel room. If she had it to do again she would stay there another few days, wait until the storm came and went, and none of this would be happening.

As if I had a choice. Never has felt like it.

Her knees and elbows are sore against the metal, but she presses on, getting closer to the end. She sees well enough for her to make out a tunnel to her right, which she assumes covers the units and runs the length of them, and a larger grate up ahead which leads to the roof.

For a moment she hesitates and peers down the dark shaft to her right. *Don't think about the movie Alien,* she tells herself. But it's too late, and images flood her mind of a doomed and panic-stricken Tom Skerritt shooting his flamethrower down the shaft behind him. For some reason this makes her chuckle but she's not sure why. Is this normal, simply nerves, or is she really losing it this time?

She lights the Zippo again and holds it out in front of her.

The first few feet of the shaft are illuminated. Beyond it, shadows and night. Satisfied there's nothing hiding in the darkness, she's just about to snap the lighter shut when a burst of air comes at her from deep in the shaft. But this is different than the air moving through the system. Warmer. Thicker. And it is accompanied by what sounds like a heavy and deliberate exhale of breath. Yet as it passes through her Greer shivers uncontrollably.

What's that old saying some people use when they shiver for no apparent reason? She thinks a moment, her mind and heart racing. *Someone just walked over my grave.*

She waits, frozen in the shaft, the flames licking the metal over her head as her labored breath echoes all around her.

Trust me, he can smell you from miles away.

Greer listens. Is there something there, just beyond her range of vision, hiding in the darkness, something barely audible in the otherwise dead silence of the shaft?

He can see your nightmares while you sleep.

Whispers? Can she hear very faint whispers coming from the depths of the shaft? She strains to listen, the flame dancing now in her trembling grasp.

He can hear your darkest thoughts when you're awake.

Or is it only her own breathing she hears, reverberating back to her?

They draw him to you.

Visions of his face flash before her eyes, shielded in shadow, so close to her own out on the road, that enormous blade pressed to her throat.

Defiantly, Greer snaps the Zippo shut and continues past the dark shaft and up the slope to the roof. Ignoring awful sensations of something flying up the shaft behind her that slither from her lower back, up her spine, and into the back of her skull, she struggles closer to the grate that will get her onto the motel roof, out of this metal box and hopefully one step closer to whoever Kit Piper is.

In the quiet of the darkened office, Luke watches snow spatter against the glass wall before him. Between darkness and the increasing snowfall, visibility is reduced to a few feet at most. The highway they were able to see just moments before is now lost in a tangle of whirling snowflakes and deepening night. And somewhere out there, Evil waits. "Wind's picking up," he says softly. "And the snow's getting heavier."

Behind him, just barely visible in the sparse candlelight, Doc leans against the front desk, shotgun in hand and a cigarette dangling from his lips. "Storm's gonna get a hell of a lot worse before it gets better."

"I don't want to die."

The words hit Doc like an anvil. He's heard them so many times over so many years, usually by those who not long after they speak them are dead and gone. He tries to forget, but in times like these their hopeless faces return to him, and he remembers. Men. Women. Children. He remembers them all, each and every one. He takes a final drag on his cigarette, drops it, steps on it. "I know."

"Things went to shit with my girl." Luke pulls off his knit hat, stuffs it into his raincoat pocket and runs a hand over his head. It comes back slick with perspiration. "I fucked my life up bad, you know? Just a few hours ago I was so down I thought maybe...maybe I didn't want to live, maybe it'd be better if I died. I thought about coming to a motel like this and just doing myself. Who'd care, right? What difference would it make?"

"He feels it in you."

"Feels what?"

"Your sorrow, the hopelessness. He feeds off it."

He looks back at Doc. One side of the older man's weathered face is cloaked in darkness, the other awash in candlelight. "You really a doctor?"

"Used to be."

"What kind?"

"Surgeon."

"No shit?"

"No shit."

"Making the big bucks, right?"

"Not anymore. Not in a long time."

"You just chase him?"

Doc nods.

"He killed your family?"

"My wife and daughter."

"How'd it happen?"

"I don't really talk about it."

"I feel you. Just trying to understand some of this shit, that's all."

Doc stares straight ahead, as if in a trance. "After college I took some time off, bummed around a while. Went to medical school late, so I ended up getting married and being a father later than most. Waited my whole life for my family, and he took them away from me."

"Always wanted a family," Luke tells him sullenly.

"Yeah. Me too."

"What was it like?"

"What?"

"Being a dad."

"Best thing in the world. But my daughter was just a little girl when The Dealer found us."

"Is he really everything you say he is?"

Doc swallows the rage, does his best to wrestle it back into something he can control and handle. "He cut her tongue out of her head and ate it right in front of her. Then he slit her throat from ear to ear and raped her while she bled out on our kitchen floor, her mother's body gutted and beheaded not ten feet away. Her name was Jodie. She was nine years old."

For the second time that evening, Luke finds the crucifix around his neck and clutches it for comfort. "How'd you survive?"

"I died that day too."

"You know what I mean. Why'd he spare you?"

"He didn't. Wasn't me he wanted... it was them. He shot me once in the chest, once in the stomach, figured I'd be dead soon enough. But I lived. Was all over the news, cops swore they'd get the killer, bunch of politicians paraded around saying justice would be done, but he was long gone, just like always, and they had nothing. I did almost a year in the hospital, another year in physical rehab. Then I learned everything I could about him, about the markings he'd left behind all over our house, his rituals, what they meant and what they led to. I liquidated everything. We had a good amount of money ahead of us as it was, so I took off, traveled the country tracking him, trying to find him, learning more and more the harder I looked, the deeper underground I went. That's when I learned how this life really works, what's real and what isn't. I keep going for my wife and child, for all the others over all the years. And I won't stop until he kills me, or I end him. I've been living off old money for years. Won't last much longer, but now I know it won't have to. It's all been leading up to this."

Luke moved closer, his face stern and tight in the darkness. "We need to kill this motherfucker. Tonight."

Can't kill something that's never been alive. But we can stop it.

Doc gazes up at the vent then closes his eyes. In the darkness of his mind he sees blood, fire, smoke and black magic...the cards falling from The Dealer's bloody hands, spiraling down into darkness, into a pit of screams where souls go to die and await their master.

And somewhere nearby, hidden in the snow and wind and boundless night, Doc hears the faintest trace of musical chanting, like the Gregorian chants he loves so much and listens to when he's alone and quiet. These are not the growls of demons but the breathtaking songs of angels, a choir of ancient warriors, a helpless tribunal bound by ancient decrees to watch the struggles of Man without intervening unless otherwise instructed to do so. They watch these poor, relatively helpless creatures, unequipped to battle the darkness as they can, left to their own devices in a world gone mad, knowing that only a select few can truly hear them sing their beautiful hymns while they await their chance to bludgeon and destroy those who seek to topple *their* master.

The sound is so beautiful it makes Doc want to weep. But even in beauty there is violence, madness. The line between the divine and the damned, the living and the dead and the real and the imagined, is often painfully thin.

"It's bigger than all of us," Doc says. "Whether we want it to be or not."

Luke nods, though he doesn't fully understand and probably never will.

I wish you could hear it too, Doc thinks.

Memories come to him, beautiful memories of his wife Karen and their daughter Jodie. He crushes them, sweeps them back into the darkness from which they came.

There is work to be done, destruction to be wrought.

He clutches the shotgun, holds on tight and watches the storm grow more powerful and deadly with each passing second.

THIRTEEN

reer manages to push the grate free and drop it down without making too much noise. She hopes the wind helps to mask the sound as she climbs through and drops down onto the roof. Her palms hit the cold slushy snow and she slides down onto her knees, the wetness seeping through her jeans and sending a chill through her entire body. There's already at least three or four inches of snow accumulated on the roof. The freezing air hits her like a slap to the face as tiny particles of ice ride the snowflakes and tickle her eyes. The flakes are so big and blowing about with such ferocity that she cannot see more than a few feet in front of her. Above her, patches of black sky slip through the curtains of snow, reminding her again how dark it's become. She scrambles up into a crouch and tries her best to get a look at the roof. It's not terribly large but is cluttered with other vents and utility units. Hunched over, she hurries along the center of the roof toward the next closest structure; a large vent she quickly realizes is a heating duct, as hot air leaks from it in a steady wave. It makes perfect sense. If one were to hide up here under such conditions, this is the logical choice, perhaps the only choice where one could survive the elements.

Trying to remain low as possible, Greer moves carefully around the sizeable vent, squinting through the snow and pawing at her eyes as she circles around it. Just as she reaches the backside she hears a quiet high-pitched grunt followed by a flash of something dark coming at her through the snow and darkness.

It isn't until it makes impact with her chest and vaults her away and onto her back that she realizes someone wearing a fairly rugged boot has kicked her. She lay in the snow stunned and trying to catch her breath, the flakes tumbling down at her like beautiful swirling razors. She feels her hair becoming wet, and bits of icy snow sliding along her neck. Her hands are cold and stiff, but she remembers the knife Doc gave her, and as she rolls over onto all fours, she grips its handle.

Through the storm, Greer sees a small female figure stumbling across the roof toward the lower, longer roof in the distance that runs the length of the units. She can't call out, but knows if she doesn't stop her she may never get another chance to save her. *Visibility is bad wherever he is too*, she thinks, and risking it, Greer stands and breaks into a full run, determined to catch Kit before she drops off this roof and onto the other.

She knows she won't make it. "Wait!" she calls out, hoping her voice carries far enough to reach her but not enough to reach the lot below.

Kit staggers to a stop near the edge of the roof and looks back with equal parts terror and confusion.

Greer holds her hands up. "Stop," she says breathlessly, chest heaving. "It's OK, it's—I promise it's OK, I'm not—my name's Greer. I'm here to help you."

Kit's face hints at relief, or perhaps it's only disbelief, Greer cannot be certain. She stands in the whirl of snow, hands at her sides, looking drenched and freezing, her eyeglasses dotted with moisture and smeared with snow.

"There are two others down in the office," Greer says. "Come with me. Please, we can't stay out here. He'll see us."

Kit nods hesitantly, as if she doesn't quite understand but comprehends enough to know she needs to listen. "He killed Carlin," she says in a small voice.

"*Please.*" Greer reaches a hand out. "Come with me. Now."

"He...killed him."

Greer closes the gap between them with two quick strides and takes Kit's hand. It's cold as ice. "Come on, honey, it's going to be OK, but we have to get off this roof."

Kit nods again. "I...I know, I...OK."

Behind her, Greer sees something moving in the snow. At first she can't be sure what it is because it's a distance away on the roof of the units, but within seconds she can see that it's moving fast.

A silhouette running toward them...duster flapping behind him...

Greer tightens her grip on Kit's hand. "Run!" She turns and bolts back toward the vent, dragging Kit along with her. "Don't look back! Just run!"

They reach the vent quickly.

"Get back down into the office!" Greer tells her. "I'm right behind you!"

Kit climbs in and is gone.

Although she knows she shouldn't, something forces Greer to look back over her shoulder. Having just leapt from the lower roof to this one in a single bound, the man in the duster lands on the edge of the roof in a crouch, head bowed. He rises to his feet.

Everything in her being screams for her to follow Kit into that vent. But she cannot move.

He slowly raises his head. She still cannot make out his eyes.

Come to me, little lamb, as you know you want to. As you know you must. I can set you free of this world and all its horrors. Come to me, Greer. Come.

She grips the knife at her side. "How do you know my name?"

You told me your name in your dreams...your nightmares. Don't you remember, little lamb?

He pulls open the duster, holding it apart like great leather wings extended out on either side of him. And inside, things move and writhe and whip about, slimy appendages and bloody tentacles. Dark things drop free of him and scurry through the snow, rushing toward her in waves like a living blanket as his rumbling laughter cuts the night.

I can smell the blood running through you, lamb. I can taste it.

Greer turns and vaults into the vent, sliding down on her stomach into the darkness, only cognizant seconds later that something has followed her into the shaft. Several things. Small and fast and closing on her even as she crawls toward what she can only hope is at least temporary safety.

She is only a few feet into the shaft when she hears squeaking noises behind her, along with a ticking sound similar to fingers tapping a keyboard. Scrambling through the dark shaft she tries desperately to remember where she put the Zippo. As she drops down into the final length of vent she remembers and manages to pry it from her jeans pocket. Flipping it open, she flicks it on, and the tunnel is illuminated enough for her to see that Kit is already gone and most likely safe in the office with the others.

Greer continues on fast as she can, twisting and turning until she is on her back and sliding. She lifts her head, and with the aid of the flame is able to see what has followed her into the shaft.

The largest rats she has ever seen, sneering at her with their pointed teeth and glowing eyes. A wave of the creatures pour through the shaft, so many she cannot tell where one creatures ends and the other begins, all of them swarming over her even as she kicks and screams and stabs at them with the lighter.

She continues desperately backing down the shaft as they bite and claw at her, gnawing at her hands and neck and face, tearing free chunks of her flesh in agonizing bloody sprays, her screams echoing like thunder along the metal walls surrounding her. She drops the lighter, the flame is extinguished, and in darkness, she covers her eyes in the hopes of protecting them.

Sliding along, she feels their claws on her throat, their whiskers tickling her fingers, their teeth nibbling her knuckles, eating their way through her hands to her eyes. Fear has become unthinkable terror so profound her body and mind can no longer process it, and Greer feels herself starting to shut down.

But then, through the blood and darkness and excruciating pain, she sees a faint bit of flickering light. *The candle on the front desk,* her shattered mind tells her. *I'm almost there.*

"Keep an eye on the front," Doc orders, hoisting the shotgun up in one hand and reaching for the vent with the other to help guide the small young woman down.

Luke stands before the door, watches the night.

Kit Piper is disheveled, soaking wet, freezing and terrified, but appears to be physically unharmed. "It's all right," Doc tells her, taking her hand as she drops down onto the front desk and then to the floor.

Screams follow from deep inside the shaft, and Greer's kicking reverberates out through the open grate like drumbeats. Kit stumbles over to the far wall and squats down, hugging herself as Doc cocks his head for a better look up into the vent.

"Greer!" he calls out. "Keep moving! Just keep moving!"

What is only seconds but feels like hours pass, and finally Greer appears at the edge of the opening, still lying on her back. She spins and falls out, landing hard on the front desk before rolling off onto the floor, swatting and kicking and flailing about in a panic.

"Get them off! G-Get them off get them off!"

Doc climbs onto the desk, swings shut the grate then hops back down as Luke turns from the door and tries to figure out what Greer is reacting to.

"There's nothing there," Doc tells her. He lays the shotgun on the desk and grabs hold of her by her shoulders. "Greer, look at me. *Look* at me!"

She does, eyes wide with terror and her entire body trembling.

"There's nothing there. It's not real. Whatever he's showing you isn't real. Look. Look, there's nothing there, nothing on you."

Greer inspects herself as if for the first time, and her horror becomes confusion and disbelief. "But I...I saw them, I...I *felt* them." She looks at Doc helplessly. "Rats. Hundreds of them, they...they were all over me."

"It's all right now. You're all right."

"He's in my head, isn't he?"

"Fuck is this shit?" Luke mumbles.

Doc looks away, turns to Kit. "Miss, are you all right?"

"I think so." Kit pulls her glasses off, wipes the lenses with her shirttail then slides them back on and looks around, able to truly see again. She points to Greer. "You saved my life. I'm sorry I kicked you."

Greer touches her chest, as if to make certain that pain is real.

"When I heard someone coming I closed my eyes and kicked when you sounded close. I never even saw you until you called out and I looked back." Kit slowly gets to her feet. "If you hadn't stopped me I would've run right into him."

"How long have you been up there?" Luke asks.

"Seems like forever. The man out there killed Carlin. He really killed him."

"Who's Carlin?"

"He works...worked here with me. I work the front desk nights. We'd just switched shifts and Carlin was on his way out when...I knew I had to get out of here and the only other way out fast was into the shaft. I didn't think he'd be able to fit. Eventually I went up on the roof and hid, I—I didn't know what to do. I didn't have time to get my jacket or my keys and I knew with the storm I wouldn't get far on foot so I just..." Kit's horrified gaze slowly glides between them, one to the next. "What's happening? I...I can't believe this."

"We don't know that much either," Greer says, her nerves evening out. "Just that there's a maniac out there trying to kill us."

"There's only one of us that has any real answers to all this," Luke announces. "Ain't that right, Doc?"

Doc responds by introducing himself and the others to Kit.

She shakes their hands in turn. "Kit Piper."

Luke slips into the office, grabs her army jacket and holds it up for her so she can slip into it. "Here, you're shivering."

"Thanks," she says, wrapping herself up tight in the jacket. She notices the papers all over the floor. "My manuscript."

"You a writer?"

She shrugs. "Hopefully one day I will be."

Greer paces about like a trapped lioness walking her cage. "It's time we got some answers, Doc. You need to tell us exactly what the hell is going on here. Because what I saw out there, what I just experienced isn't possible."

"There's a chance we could all die tonight," Luke says. "Don't you think if we do we deserve to know why?"

Doc retrieves the shotgun, holds it by his side and watches the snow come down awhile. The wind howls like the tortured soul it is, shaking the motel and sweeping waves of white about the lot and across the front of the building.

Somewhere far away, beneath the wind, Doc can still hear the beautiful chants, the ethereal songs of angels rolling across the heavens. But he hears laughter too, the guttural laughter of the thing on the roof waiting to sate its hunger, its need. *Heaven and Hell, hand-in-hand as always,* he thinks, *all of us slaves to both, forever caught between darkness and the light.*

"He's in human form," Doc says softly, "but only because he has to be. Underneath it all he's a serpent, a child of the land of the dead. He's the thing we fear the most as children. As adults we try to convince ourselves his kind don't exist, *can't* exist. But all the while, you know deep down he really *is* under your bed."

Doc closes his eyes, sees it all...the carnage...the beginning...the end.

"I've been tracking him for years," he says. "I call him The Dealer."

FOURTEEN

Six years ago, my life ended. It died the day he walked into our lives and slaughtered my wife and little girl. I was thirty-four years old when my daughter Jodi was born, maybe a little older than most, but my marriage and family came a bit later for me than most too. I was forty-three when they died…when The Dealer took them from me. Before Karen and Jodi, I was lost. Born and raised in Wyoming, I grew up dirt poor in a little shack of a house with my mother, father and three sisters. Had to work and scrape for everything. Watched my old man break his back working as a laborer for peanuts. Watched my mother on her hands and knees scrubbing floors for even less. And watched them both drink themselves into oblivion. I worked hard at school, got scholarships. Went to college then medical school, became a doctor, a surgeon. No more problems. I had it all. The big house, the summer condo, nice cars, every toy and luxury I could ever want. And none of it meant a goddamn thing. Then I met Karen, and everything changed. My life made sense, and for the first time I didn't feel lost and alone anymore. When Jodi was born I felt love and a sense of family I never even knew existed. We were so happy, all of us, respectable, decent people raising our child and living our lives. Never occurred to me it could all fall apart so easily. I dealt with death and the fragility of human life every day, but I never thought it'd touch me, or those I loved. Foolish, I know, but that's what happiness does to you. Blinds you in the best possible way. Karen had struggled with some mental health issues since she'd been a child, but she was on medication that helped control it. When she started to become depressed I blamed it on the meds not working. What I didn't realize was that I'd become complacent and, much as I loved them, took her and Jodi for granted. That car out there, the Bel Air, it was my baby. Fixing and restoring old cars has always been a hobby of mine. I spent hours in the garage working on that thing, finding the parts, restoring it and bringing it back to life. That's what I did, I brought things back to life, whether on an operating table or in a garage. Took me more than two years to finish it. All those hours spent fiddling with that car when I could've been with my family. It's why I still drive it, so I'll never forget that I'd give it all back for even five minutes with them. I just didn't see it then. I couldn't understand how Karen could've been unhappy. We had a great life and loving family. How could anything be wrong?

And my God, how I adored her. How I adored them both.

Without warning, The Dealer brought it all down. He came out of nowhere, and suddenly we were in Hell and this thing was butchering my family. He shot me, left me for dead and destroyed Karen and Jodi. It's not enough for him to simply kill. It's a ritual for The Dealer, a rite. A massacre. I didn't know that then, all I saw was a madman killing my family right before my eyes.

Once I was out of the hospital and had gotten through the physical therapy and was strong again, I went back to school, but not one of healing. This time, I learned how to end life rather than save it. I hired a weapons and hand-to-hand-combat expert, learned everything I could from him, trained constantly and absorbed the knowledge I needed. In my downtime, I researched and learned everything I could about magic—black and white—and what his demonic marks and spells and rituals meant. I learned how to read most, and how to fight them. It's all I did, day and night, for more than a year. Then I sold everything except for that car and the clothes on my back and headed out after him. I've been tracking him ever since. Six years. Six years of death, mayhem and evil, always one step ahead of me but so close I could almost reach out and touch him. I've been so close sometimes the bodies are still warm. I almost had him three years ago in a little desert town in Nevada. Came close in New Orleans too, right after the floods, but he slipped through and got away, bodies in his wake as usual.

In the years on the road I've learned even more. I've met with Shamans, White and Black Magic Witches, Voodoo

Priests and Priestesses, Seers, preachers, mediums, monks, hardcore Satanists—you name it—everyone in the world of the occult, from practitioners to professors, I've talked to them all. I've picked their brains. And all the while, I've tracked him across the country and even through Canada and Mexico. If this storm hadn't trapped us both, he'd have left the continent soon. I think he had his eye on Central then South America. Not that he hasn't been there before, he's been everywhere before. Wherever there's life, he's left behind death. It's what he does. It's what he is.

To find him, to track him and to eventually stop him, you have to believe in things you're told don't exist, things that are only believed by the ignorant or the wildly misguided religious sorts. Problem is, the things they believe are wrong, but the things they believe exist...do. The Dealer's one of them. He remains in human form because he has to in order to move about our world in any physical sense. He hides inside us, within the flesh, but he is not of the flesh. He's not human. Never has been. He's spirit. A demon, a ghost, makes no difference what you call him. He has many names in many cultures, but it's all the same. Evil is a disease of humanity. No one's immune, no one escapes.

Landscapes, faces, cultures, beliefs, they all change, but he remains the same. He may wear something different, or move from one human host to another, but it's all window-dressing. Unchanged in thousands of years, he's been here since the earliest times, since the dawning. But time is different for his kind. There is no aging or decay. It passes differently for him. A day for him is years for us. Unless he's stopped or the curse is lifted, he'll be here until the world is a wasteland, until all conscious life has vanished from the face of the Earth. Then he can return to the land of the dead. His world. His home. And there, with all the souls he's collected over all the years, he becomes a god. Until then, he's trapped here, cursed to roam and slaughter through his blood rituals and demonic sacrifices. A nomadic killer from an ancient history and a reality discarded as fairytale long ago, he has one purpose. Destruction. It's the despair that lures him, the sorrow and the pain. The hopelessness. He feeds on it the same as we take in oxygen, because he has known God. He's spoken His name, served Him. He is of The Fallen. And when his kind fell, they fell for good. There's no turning back. Not then. Not now. Not ever.

He always kills, but usually not in such numbers so close together. In the past it wasn't necessary, and in certain situations too dangerous. He likes to follow storms and natural disasters, where it's easier to kill and where often many disappearances and deaths will be blamed on the events. In New Orleans, after the floods, he was on a rampage. He killed in numbers I'd never seen before. Now he's ramping it up and on a spree again. Maybe the curse is coming to an end, or maybe he knows there's no way out and this time it's him or me.

Few years back, I was tracking him through the west. I was on Highway 50 in Nevada. They call it 'The Loneliest Road in America.' Once you're on it you know why. Parallels the old Pony Express trail. You can go forever without seeing another car or living soul. I found myself out there one night driving my way through. The Dealer was ahead of me and I was pretty sure he was headed into Utah. I hadn't slept in days and the road was putting me to sleep. I'd made a lot of contacts with the underground by then, and wherever I went, one person into the occult would know another and tell me who to talk to whenever I got somewhere else. There's a loose network if you know who to talk to, and if they want to help you. Most knew what The Dealer was and didn't want him in their midst any more than I did. But way out there on 50, it was just the two of us, all of our sins, and that endless road.

It's the first time I heard the singing. Like Gregorian chants, so beautiful and moving, yet so unsettling at the same time. Nothing human could produce such beautiful sounds. We had tried over the centuries, and we'd come close, but never with anything that echoed forth as if resonating from some impossibly giant hall. It was a sound that made you cry like a baby. Not in fear, but joy.

I listened to the angels sing their ancient musical chants, and they led me off the road. I pulled over and began to walk out into the desert. It was night and pitch-black, no moon. But I could see. Somehow, I could see. I walked through the darkness until I came upon a small trailer about a mile or so in. At first it didn't look like anyone still lived there, that maybe it had been abandoned a few years prior. But when I got up close and saw the lanterns burning, I realized there was an old woman sitting there in a rickety lawn chair. Huddled up in a threadbare blanket, she wore a kerchief on her head that did little to distract from the tangled mess of white tendrils that was her hair. She looked right at me, but her eyes were gray and thick with cataracts, and her skin hung from her frail skeleton like slabs of rotting dough. She rested both hands on an old walking stick carved from knotty wood. She wore rings of silver on every finger of her gnarled, arthritis-savaged hands, numerous silver bracelets on her wrists that jingled when she moved, and a filthy skirt that reached her ankles. On her feet were tattered sandals.

'Been waitin' on you.' The woman claimed she'd called me to her. That she'd 'seen' me, seen what I was doing, what I was pursuing, and had brought me to her so that she could help me better understand. She explained she'd been born blind but with a 'second' sight. 'You ain't the light,' she told me in a raspy, weak voice. "But you ain't the dark neither. Not yet.'

'Who are you?'

'Just a guide, a messenger, nothin' more.'

Things howled and moved in the night behind her, beyond her trailer. She seemed unconcerned; her deeply wrinkled and weathered face set like stone.

'All he has is memories, same as you,' she told me. 'Real or not, don't matter. The nightmares, the blood, that's what matters. And the game. Cards don't mean nothin', not really. More a prop, see? But he's always playin' that game. Even when he ain't.'

I'd seen the cards he sometimes left behind, and I'd even seen the tattoos on his arms—I'd been that close once—but never understood what they meant.

'You playin' too, just don't know it.' She blinked, gray eyes staring straight ahead, seeing nothing...and everything. "We all playin' it, and we all playin' alone. Only way to play solitaire, see? Same way we come into the world, same way we leave it. Alone, and in the dark.

'The cards got a history, like everything else. Way back, they called them the Devil's Picture Book. They had to do with gambling and fortunetellin', so they was evil, see? To this day, you won't never see no real fisherman or miner carry a deck of cards with them to the ocean or down below.

'But them that knows better knows cards is like everything else. Good and bad. They been used to pray and foresee for just as long as they been used for evil. At the end, it don't mean nothin'. Only them usin' the cards has meanin'.'

'Why did you bring me here? What do I care about his playing cards and games of solitaire?'

'They're his comfort,' she told me. 'The cards all got meanin' to him in his sick head, got purpose in his rituals. The game ain't for real but it's a symbol just like the ones he paints on walls in human blood. It's him, alone in the night, turning...falling...just like them cards...some to good...some to bad...all of them movin' the game forward. Dealer either wins or gets trapped in the cards and has to start again. Either way, he'll just keep playin' 'til somebody stops him. Stop him, stop the game.'

'Am I the one?' I asked her.

She nodded, leaning heavier on her walking stick. 'I seen you in dreams, on the highways. I seen you in the snow...a snow full of blood, steaming guts all across it... and him... waitin'... waitin' on you.'

'I hear things.'

'I know you do.'

'Ancient songs.'

'They're prayers.'

'What do they mean?'

'What you think they mean?'

A hot wind blew up from the desert, moving through the darkness to the camp and the sparse light from the lanterns around the trailer. The air was thick and hard to breathe, full of dust and sand. Like Hell, I thought. Must be what it's like to breathe the air in Hell.

'He ain't the only one. Neither is you.'

'Why me?'

'Just the way things is. The way it's always been and how things is always gonna be. Least 'til there ain't nothin' left. We are as it's written, and round and round the heavens and hells go, see? Forever and ever. Amen.'

'What if I fail?'

'Won't be the first.' The old woman turned her head like she'd heard something off in the darkness, but her dead eyes remained forward, as if she could see me. 'But I dreamed you was the last. Remember the game. We all cards, see? All with our places. Where we got to be. Can't play red to red or black to black. God made the game, made all of us. Question is, who is God?'

'I don't care who God is. How do I kill this fuck?'

'You don't.'

I felt whatever little sliver of me still existed wither and die, and it took everything I had not to sink to my knees. 'I've come so far,' I told her, emotion getting the better of me. 'Been through so much, I...'

'Flesh is for killin'.' A dark tongue slowly protruded from her mouth and licked her pale, thin lips. 'Spirit, you got to bind.'

I closed my eyes, felt something drop into the palm of my hand. Until then I hadn't even realized I'd been holding it out for her. In my grasp, attached to the end of a black satin cord, was a clear crystal roughly the size of a golf ball. The weapon that could stop him, the only weapon, short of a sword at the hip of an angelic warrior the likes of which still sang to me from the night, their divine choir consecrating all that had taken place and what was still to come.

'Can you hear them?' I asked the old woman.

'Can you?'

'Yes.'

'But do you hear? Listen,' she said, bringing a twisted hand to her chest and pointing a crooked finger at her heart. 'Here.'

'How will I know?'

'You'll know. Same way he does. He's startin' to remember his past, and that means the curse is weakenin' and he's almost home. Hell's callin' him. You gonna stop him, you got to do it before he gets there.'

I woke up hours later in my car, miles from where I thought I'd been. I thought it was just another nightmare, but the crystal was there on the seat next to me. It was real. Everything that had led me to that point and everything that would happen from then on out. All of it was real. My wife and child weren't coming back, and The Dealer wasn't going to stop killing until I bound and imprisoned him in his own evil and madness.

Maybe then—and only then—I'd have some peace. And those beautiful voices of the angels might become a welcome, a chance at transcendence and a return to something close to the promise of the life I'd once had. Not here, but somewhere else. Somewhere better, where Karen and Jodi waited for me.

Just like I'd been told in the desert, we were all playing the game, all using our own rituals. But you can't play red on red or black on black. Spirit kills flesh. Flesh binds spirit.

There are rules. So it is written.

The old desert witch was right. Now I had to hope her magic was too.

FIFTEEN

They stand watching Doc, taking it all in, doing their best to process the impossible. Wind blows snow against the glass. Accumulating now, it creeps slowly up the front of the building. Beyond, in the lot, the cars are now covered.

"I'm so sorry for your family," Greer says softly.

He doesn't say the words, but Doc's expression reveals his appreciation.

"How do I reconcile this with my own beliefs?" Kit asks, eyes behind her glasses wide with bewilderment and dread. "I don't believe in these things."

Luke points to the roof. "I don't think he much gives a shit."

"Doesn't matter what you believe." Doc lights a cigarette, smokes it steadily, manically. "It's beyond that now. It's down to living or dying."

"Isn't it always?" Greer says. Distracted, she moves toward the front counter and peers up at the vent. "From the moment we realize we're alive?"

Before Doc can respond Luke says, "So you got this thing that can—what'd you call it—*bind* him? Then let's do it."

After another quick drag, Doc exhales through his nose, drops the cigarette to the floor and steps on it. "Not quite that easy."

"Why not?"

"The binding has to be done up close. He's not going to just stand there and submit to it. He'll fight with everything he has, and that's a lot."

Kit notices Greer studying the vent but says nothing. Instead she begins retrieving her manuscript pages from the floor and front desk and gathering them into a stack.

"What if you don't make it?" Luke asks. "What if he takes you down first? You need to show us how to do it, just in case."

"Did any of you hear that?" Greer asks, still gazing up at the vent.

The others stare at her.

"Whispers. I can hear him, he...he's whispering my name." She points to the vent. "From there."

"He wants you to listen." Doc moves between Greer and the counter, reaches out and gently touches her shoulder. "Don't."

She searches his face for some measure of how to do that. "You really can't hear it? None of you can?"

"No matter what he says, don't listen."

As Greer moves back over to the front wall, Kit nervously stuffs her manuscript pages into the knapsack, then begins collecting the items strewn across the couch and floor that were emptied from it earlier. "I smoked a blunt a while ago. Keep hoping it's like the best weed *ever* and this is all a drug trip, right? Because I really don't know what to do here, I am totally not equipped for this kind of thing. I still can't believe it's actually happening."

"Hiding here has been a temporary solution from the start," Doc explains. "He hasn't tried to get in, but he will, and we have to move before that happens. Because once he decides he's coming, there'll be no stopping him."

Kit drops her knapsack onto the couch. "Where are we supposed to go?"

"We need to—"

"What we need to do," Luke interrupts, "is stop running and hiding and start fighting. If you've got what you need to stop this fucker then do it. Up close, far away, whatever, let's take this piece of shit down while we got the numbers."

"First he needs to be trapped." Doc reaches into his jacket pocket and pulls out the talisman he told them about, a crystal roughly the size of a golf ball dangling from the end of a black satin cord. "Then he can be bound."

"And that's gonna do it?"

"You better hope so, because it's the only chance we have."

Kit sighs. "Tell me you're kidding. I have pretty much the same thing in my car hanging from the rearview. Somehow I'm thinking the key to stopping evil in the universe doesn't boil down to a trinket some kid made in China I bought at a kiosk for three dollars."

Ignoring her comment, he returns the crystal to his jacket pocket and asks, "Is there anything more to this property? Any other buildings, maybe out back or nearby?"

Greer suddenly seems as fascinated with the glass front wall as she was with the vent just seconds before. She reaches out and gently presses her hands on the sheet of glass, as if seeing it for the first time.

Kit watches Greer a moment, as if to be sure of her, and then answers. "There's an old storage shed behind the office. And there's a small diner out back, but it's been closed and locked up for a couple years now."

"A diner?"

"They used to serve food here back in the day. But I guess there wasn't enough business to keep it going so they shut it down. It's just been sitting there for quite a while as I understand it."

"How many ways in?"

"Front door and a service door for deliveries in back, but the front's been locked, and the back's been bolted shut for years. It's mostly metal, with windows along the front, long wide ones, you know what I mean."

"What's the setup inside like?"

"Standard diner, I guess."

"Tables, booths, what?"

"I've only been back there once." Kit thinks a moment. "Booths and a counter with stools, kitchen in back."

"Any open floor space?"

"Some. Just inside the door. Why?"

Rather than answer Doc says, "I assume it's locked. Is there a key?"

Kit motions to the office. "There's a ring of keys in the middle desk drawer, the one with the green rubber cover is a master key, supposedly opens anything with a lock on the premises."

"We have to get back there."

"Why?" Luke asks.

"That's where we'll trap him. That's where we'll bind him."

"How long does the binding last?"

"Eternity. It imprisons him."

"He can't get out?"

"Only if someone lets him out."

"But why back there?" Luke asks. "Why not just do it here?"

"He won't fall for it here and there's no time anyway. We have to reestablish then catch him off-guard. Kit, grab me that master key. Let's get ready to move. We'll go as one."

Luke steels himself. "We're just gonna make a break for it?"

"No other way."

Doc sees what Greer is up to and already knows what she's thinking, what she's been told in whispers and strange voices slithering through her head. Although it's just dawning on her now, he's been aware of it from the start. But there's been no time to bring it up or worry about it until now. The Dealer won't stay on the roof forever.

"I don't understand," Luke says as Kit returns from the office with the key. "If the goal is to bring him to us, why not just wait here until he comes and then do it? Why risk going from one place to another?"

Doc sidles up next to Greer. "You all right?"

She shakes her head no. "This wall is almost entirely glass."

"Yes."

Greer finally tears her eyes from the wall and looks at Doc. "He's toying with us, isn't he? This really is all a game to him, isn't it?"

Doc nods.

"You blocked the threshold but...but this is glass."

"We go as one." Doc grabs his bag and the shotgun then takes Greer by the arm and pulls her clear of the front wall. "Kit, you know exactly where it is, so you lead the way. Don't hesitate, don't ask questions and don't look back. Just get us there."

"Hold on," Luke says. "If he's coming then—"

"He's not coming," Doc tells them, his jaw tight. "He's here."

Kit moves closer to the candlelight. The glow better illuminates her face, better reveals her fear. But before she can speak something appears through the darkness outside, moving at an incredible speed. It breaks through the curtains of snow and flies into and through the front wall, exploding the enormous pane and sending shards of glass spraying and raining down on the office and everyone in it.

Amidst screams, The Dealer lands near the front desk like a giant leather bird, duster flapping in the wind as snow and ice and glass showers down all around him, bringing with him the night, the storm and the evil in all three.

SIXTEEN

It's like a dream, really. The horrible dreams of children being pursued by unimaginable evil, where beauty is deadly and the night is a living, breathing entity set on devouring them. Wherever they look, a maze of plump flakes blow about, walls of snow dancing and whirling in the darkness as cloudbursts of breath billow from their mouths and nostrils in swirling plumes, their hearts crashing, lungs burning, eyes watering. And the horror, the blind panic and crippling fear only children or the doomed can truly fathom, it's there too, running along with them through the icy storm like the lethal companion it is.

The boogieman is real, and he's right on their heels.

Kit leads the way. Luke and Greer run a close second. Doc pulls up the rear, spinning and wildly firing the shotgun as he staggers out through the newly formed portal in the front of the building. A deafening boom shatters the night but is quickly swallowed by the wind. Doc cannot be sure he hit him and doesn't wait to find out. Slipping and sliding through the snow, which is now well beyond their ankles, the group runs around the corner of the office and into deeper night, the flakes coming at them as if part of some greater, more complex attack.

At first it seems Kit's promise of a safe destination is little more than a cruel joke, as darkness and snowfall conspire to make visibility virtually nil. But as they run, the rotted shell of an old car becomes visible through the tempest, and Kit yells back to them over her shoulder. Had they been able to hear, they'd have known she was telling them they were close, but due to the wind, her voice is a muffled and distorted cry in the night.

Silhouettes of two buildings, one small, the other a larger, longer, squat structure, appear through the darkness. Kit reaches the second well ahead of the others and frantically wipes the lock free of snow and ice before plunging the key into it.

Once the lock is disengaged she slams a shoulder into the door but bounces right off. She realizes then that it opens out not in, and with a violent yank, frees the door then turns to see the others filing toward her. She ushers Greer then Luke inside then squints through the snow for Doc.

He's not there.

"Where's Doc?" Greer screams to her from inside the diner.

"Doc!" Kit yells. "Doc!"

Luke returns to the open doorway, gun leveled at the night. "He doesn't show in another couple seconds he's done."

"I thought he was right behind us!" Greer cries.

And then he appears, his long silver hair flailing in the wind as he scuttles toward them, the shotgun in one hand and his nylon bag in the other.

.38 still at the ready, Luke steps back in and away from the door.

Kit joins the others inside but holds the door open. *Come on*, she thinks, dismissing visions of The Dealer jumping out of the swirling snow behind him and snatching him away to darkness. *Come on.*

As Doc finally reaches the diner he slides the bag onto the floor out in front of him and drops to his knees. Out of breath, his chest heaves and he coughs uncontrollably while Luke pulls the door closed and Kit quickly locks it.

The others crouch or squat down alongside Doc in the dark. Wet, cold and exhausted, even once his coughing spell has stopped no one speaks. The only sound is their collective labored breath.

Outside, the storm fights to get in. But there is no sign of The Dealer.

His coughing under control, Doc scrambles for his bag. He rifles through it until he finds a large piece of chalk then sets to work on the floor just inside the door. "Make sure the place is secure best you can," he says, still trying to catch his breath.

"Can't see shit in here," Luke snaps, crawling toward the front windows. "If you got any more of those candles, get one going."

"Check the back," Doc orders, furiously drawing on the floor with his chalk.

Using Doc's Zippo, Greer and Kit stumble through the diner, around the counter and into the back through a swinging door. The kitchen is empty but for debris on the floor and some old chairs and boxes piled in the far corner. Just beyond a walk-in freezer is the back door, which they find to be secure and locked tight.

"All set," Kit says.

"And there's no other way in?"

"Only the windows, and he'll have to break those first."

"Doesn't seem to have any problems with that." Greer's face, barely visible in the flame from the lighter, peers at her through the darkness. "I don't see how we're any safer here than we were back there, but I'm trusting Doc knows what he's talking about."

"What choice do we have?"

Greer nods. "We better get back out there."

Ironically, it is the sound of shattering glass that sends them running back out into the main area of the diner. The lighter goes out, plunging them into total darkness even before they pass through the swinging door behind the counter.

"Get down!" Doc screams.

Despite the darkness they can see snow exploding through the front door and feel the wind as it cuts through the diner. The glass in the door has been blown out and lies in shards on the floor and along one of the booths. Holding hands, Kit and Greer drop to the floor as another shot booms above the shrieking wind and a corner of the lunch counter blows apart.

Luke crawls to the opening, gets up on his knees and fires the .38 into the night, squeezing off four rounds before falling back behind the closest booth.

More shots ring out in the night, the shooter invisible in the storm but the results of his attack appearing as pops and little explosions across the diner each time a round hits.

Kit and Greer crawl behind the counter as Doc, still lying flat on the floor, inches his way toward his shotgun, which he left a few feet away. Once he's got it he rolls over onto his back, swings his legs around and braces the butt of the shotgun on his upper thigh, pumps and fires out through the door into the night.

The moment the shots cease, Doc calls out to the others. "Is everyone all right?"

Kit and Greer answer yes, and Luke responds with, "We should've never come back here. We're trapped here too. I only got a couple rounds left."

"We need to block the door." Doc gets to his knees and squints, doing his best to see in the dark. At the far end of the diner are some old tables and chairs stacked atop one another and thrown into a pile. *Better than nothing.* "Greer and Kit, help me with the door. Stay low. Luke!" He tosses him the shotgun.

In one fluid motion, Luke catches it and spins toward the door, watching the night and ready to fire if need be.

Greer and Kit join Doc, and together they scurry over to the pile of discarded furniture. The tables are largest and heaviest, so they pull down two of them and slide them across the floor to the doorway. Doc tips the first and they throw the second on top. After two more trips, two tables and several chairs fill the doorway, the pile nearly halfway up the doorframe. Snow continues to blow in through the open space up top, and in the time it took to move the furniture the first several feet of floor just inside the diner are covered with a layer of snow. Unfortunately the makeshift blockade does little to slow the wind, and the temperature inside the diner continues to plummet.

Without warning the thunderous shots return and the diner windows begin blowing out one by one, shattering and spraying the dining room as everyone dives for cover.

Then abruptly as they began, the shots cease, and there is only the storm, the wind and the cold.

After a moment everyone begins to move, to inspect themselves and make sure they're all right. Luke hurries to a booth, slides onto the bench and peeks out through the now open space that had been a window. He looks back, tosses the shotgun to Doc. "If he has all this power why is he fucking around with this bullshit? Why doesn't he just rush us like he did back at the office?"

"He's not indestructible," Doc manages, crawling toward the counter. Once there he sits down with his back against it and begins reloading his shotgun. "He's trapped in human form. The body will withstand more than most normal people would but if he stays in a wounded host too long the body will die or become useless like any other."

"And then he jumps to someone else?" Greer asks. "A new host?"

"It's not that easy. It's not like the movies where a demon just slides in and out of people at will. He has to be allowed in. He's already searching for a new place to hide, trust me."

Kit removes her eyeglasses, quickly wipes them off. "Inside one of *us*?"

"That's why if you hear him talking to you, don't listen."

Hands to her head, Greer grimaces not in pain but horror. "But I *did* hear him. Before, whispering through the vent, he—"

"Like I told you, ignore it. Think about something else. Pray. Whatever works, just don't listen. Don't engage it. Fight it. *Resist*."

"OK." Greer nods, draws a deep breath and tries to put on a strong face, but it's obvious she's just barely clinging to control. "OK."

"Snow's coming in fast," Luke says. "And the temperature's dropping. We stay here we'll freeze to death."

"You wanted to fight and make a stand." Doc racks the shotgun. "Well here it is."

"Yeah but if he's going to play games and try to wait and freeze us out then we need make a move now. We need to go get the bastard."

"He has to come to us."

"Maybe he's too smart for that."

"Maybe he is. We'll find out."

Luke looks back. "So we sit and wait? Seriously?"

"Seriously."

"He don't get us," Luke mumbles, "the storm will."

"I think I'd rather take my chances in the storm," Greer says.

Kit hugs herself against the cold. "Luke might have a point. We can't just huddle here indefinitely. Sooner or later we *will* freeze to death, and in these temperatures I think we're talking a few hours at most."

"Quiet," Luke says, inching closer to the jagged bottom of the window. "I just saw him moving around out there. Something...I...saw something moving in the snow, it..."

Through the whiteout, a figure slips free, moving between the flakes with an odd gait. Luke squints, watching, unable to look away now, rising higher on his knees in the booth for a better view. It's not possible and yet...there it is.

"What is it?" Greer presses.

"Can't," Luke mutters, "can't be, it...can't."

But it is, Luke. It is real and right here in front of you. Look and see for yourself, lamb. This is the future I can give you. You can have it all back again, and this time it can be right, just the way you've always imagined it. You and Rachel and the child you've always wanted.

Skipping...the figure is a child and she's...she's skipping...

Emotion wells in him the likes of which he has never before known. Somewhere between rage and sorrow, he rises up and levels the .38 out at the storm and the lies coming toward him.

"Luke, get down!" Doc screams. "Get down, don't look, he's—"

A daughter, Luke, a beautiful baby girl...

As the phantom child vanishes in the flakes, Luke can see and hear only Rachel and the life he let slip through his fingers, the life he wasted. The gun is heavy in his hand, too heavy suddenly, and like in a dream where everything looks and feels as if one has stumbled into a funhouse hall of mirrors, where all is distorted and dizzy and illusory, he cannot lift it or fire it or even focus his eyes on the world around him.

"Rachel?" he whispers. "Baby?"

Come to me, lamb, everything will be all right if you just come to me.

Doc crawls across the floor toward the booth fast as he can.

He's too late.

Just above the howling wind comes the swooshing sound of velocity followed by the thump of impact.

Something bursts from the center of Luke's back, effortlessly ripping through him and the raincoat, protruding like an impossibly long accusatory finger.

Doc stops short, stays low. There is nothing he can do now, and he knows it. Somewhere behind him in the dark Greer gasps and cries out and Kit says something too, and although he can hear them their words are garbled and lost in the madness and fear, the helplessness.

Slowly, Luke turns to face the others. Still on his knees on the booth bench, he steadies himself with his free hand against the table, eyes wide with disbelief and shock, mouth open but silent. The arrow has gone clear through him, the aluminum shaft glistening against the snowflakes. He looks straight ahead but sees nothing more of this world. He's already trudging toward the next, focused on things the others can neither see nor understand.

Someone screams "No!" and there is crying. Someone pleads for Doc to somehow help him.

But no one moves.

Another arrow bursts out through the base of Luke's throat like a special effect in a horror movie. His body bucks but remains upright, and he makes a soft guttural sound that emanates from deep inside him.

Doc lunges forward onto one knee, the shotgun aimed at the window.

The .38 slips from Luke's grasp, hits the table and falls to the floor as a third arrow explodes through his chest. This time he gasps and grunts, and a ribbon of dark blood sprays from his mouth, arcs in the air and splashes the booth.

Wind slams the diner, and as Luke's eyes roll back to white, he finally falls. Backwards. Tumbling out through the window, his body momentarily snags on the jagged remnants of glass along the bottom of the frame before sliding out and away into the storm with a horrifying ripping sound.

Doc pops up to his feet and fires repeatedly into the night, unable to see anything beyond the furious snowfall but continuing until the shotgun is empty. As he drops back down and begins to reload, a shadow glides by him.

It isn't until she's scooped up the .38 and with a primal scream fired the last two shots at the storm that he realizes it is Greer.

The gun clicks empty, but she keeps pulling the trigger.

Doc reaches up, grabs the waistband of her jeans and yanks her down to the floor with him. Kit scrambles closer, and the three wait.

The fury of the storm rages on, offering nothing, its secrets hidden in darkness and blood.

SEVENTEEN

As The Dealer drags Luke's body back across the lot by the ankles, he focuses not on the kill or the rituals that must follow, but the tranquility *inside* the storm, where there is no wind or snow or sleet, no blood or violence, only the final, quiet stillness of the grave. What came before, and what follows, are not yet relevant. Within the storm there is a silence the others can never know. He feels it prickling through him like electrical current, but this strange and beautiful silence does not come to those who hear it. Only those who come to *it* can hear and feel its power and splendor, those who know and understand the quiet that follows a human kill. They alone can truly comprehend that unique stitch in time where hunter and fallen prey exist together in symbiotic clarity, draped in the cloak of transference, where struggle becomes acceptance, panic becomes peace, light becomes darkness and life becomes death.

There is poetry in evil.

Back around the side of the motel office building, he releases Luke's legs and crouches down next to the knapsack he left there. Putting his crossbow aside, he retrieves his scalpel from the knapsack and begins removing the man's lips, slicing them free at the ends then peeling them back as he slides the blade beneath and works it back and forth in a sideways sawing motion, deeper and across the kill's mouth. He takes the top lip, then the bottom. It leaves Luke's face looking ghoulish and inhuman, as if his dead eyes staring into eternity and his body pierced with arrows wasn't enough. Holding them in the palm of his bloody hand, The Dealer gently presses the lips to his own and begins to pray.

A while later, when he's finished, The Dealer returns to the office. There, he removes his deck of cards from his coat pocket and places them on the front desk. After tossing his hat aside, he looks over the knit hat he took from Luke's body. It can be worn as either a regular hat or pulled down as a full ski mask. The Dealer chooses the later, placing the hat on his head then slowly stretching it down across his face until the mouth and eyeholes match up. He likes this. It reminds him of an executioner's hood.

The cards whisper to him. What he'd really like to do is sit and ride the storm out in one of the rooms with a bottle of vodka and his deck. The others will be dead by morning anyway, what difference does it make? He could easily simply let them freeze to death, but just like The Dealer, the one hunting him has a destiny. And destiny will not be ignored. It is beyond good or evil.

The Dealer touches the cards with something approaching tenderness. His peace. His escape. *Take me. Take me down into the dark where there is only the game and my mind goes quiet.*

He knows this cannot be. The game is for later. It is his reward. He cannot simply play it whenever he wishes. There are rules, and although he is weary, he knows there are more moves to make, and that in a sense, he is already playing the game, has been for quite some time. He is the dealer and the cards are his pawns. Red to black, black to red, high to low.

Bone to flesh. Flesh to blood.

Something burns deep within him. Beneath the mask his face twitches into a smile. He may never know what true joy is, but there is such pleasure in carnage, such ecstasy in agony.

He closes his eyes and remembers splitting Luke from breastbone to crotch out there in the snow. The body was still warm, the blood steaming. He remembers the sound and horrible stink as he plunged his hands into the open cavity and ripped the intestines free in a mangle of bloody wet cords. How he'd held them up to the snowy dark sky as an offering, how they'd felt as they brushed his face, hot and sticky and slick as they smeared his skin.

His erection grows, tightens his pants. He licks his lips.

Somewhere, beyond the dark skies, clouds roll, and those memories are replaced with others. Far older and more profound, they play out before his mind's eye like a film slinking through an old projector.

The sky there... he remembers that most of all because it is so different from the skies here. Neither blue nor black, neither orange nor red, it is a fantastic blend of them all, like a great canvas smeared with several haphazard brushstrokes, the clouds churning and turbulent and alive, rolling over charred and blackened hilltops where his kind, once brethren but now enemy, lie impaled on giant spires of bone protruding from the ground like blasphemous trees. Their bodies dripping blood and bile, arms and legs dangling, broken, limp and useless as their once-magnificent wings.

Before the chaos things were so different, but he can barely recall those times. They come to him sometimes, faded and blurred, lost somehow over so many years, so many tears, so much blood and horror and death. He thinks it must be similar to how elderly humans try so desperately to remember distant childhoods. There was once a time, very long ago, when he would watch the sunrise and hear the music of his home, and he would be moved as nothing else could move him. Basking in the glory of His love, he could still see true beauty then, feel it down to his core. Before darkness became his beauty. Before the wars and the death and destruction, before The Fall. He truly had been there once, hadn't he? Not the home he'd been banished to but his original home.

Although he no longer has any connection to those times, and who he was then is no more, somewhere inside he at least retains some fond memories. Doesn't he? And aren't those memories as real as anything else? As real as this body, this snow and ice and cold, this blood, these cards, his rituals and sacrifices, his rage, his nightmares. It's all so devastatingly real. Isn't it?

What if he's wrong? What if none it's real and he really is one of them?

He's so tired. It might help if he could better feel the cold.

For just a moment he wishes he could drop to his knees and cry and beg for forgiveness and a way out of this horrid darkness. He wishes he could grasp the faint glimmer of what he once knew, what he threw to the wind and has lost forever. But he cannot.

His home is in darkness, along those blackened hills where the sky is alive and roiling with terror and mayhem and the air is thick and hot and smells of death and decay, of rot.

Hell is calling. The curse is almost over, his time here almost done. But there is a final move to be made, one more drop of a card to finish the game before he can finally make his true escape. The one hunting him must die, along with the others. And then he will sit in the snow, perched along the roof of the motel, and watch the night. He will watch it recede and become daylight, and when the sun has risen in the sky, he will be no more. He will finally be gone from here. The story will be over.

So many years... so much blood... so much death and destruction... and all of it leading to this. It scarcely seems possible that his freedom could be so close. He has dreamed of this moment, and finally, it is within reach.

He will sit upon a throne of human skin and bone. He will drink their blood from a golden chalice and his slaves will gather obediently at his feet. He will again be the great warrior he once was. Revered. Feared. But never will he bow before these inferior creatures as instructed by the one who once loved his kind more than any other then took it away and gave it to *them*. He has slaughtered His precious creations for thousands of years, and now *he* will be their god, and *they* will bow before *him*, as it should be.

He pulls a bottle of vodka from his knapsack, unscrews the cap and tosses it aside. Clothes from the latest victim have already been removed and carefully torn into strips. Methodically, he prepares his deadly cocktails.

Very soon now the curse will be lifted.

Arms full, he steps into night. The storm conceals him in a sea of flakes.

I'm going home.

EIGHTEEN

T o Kit, it looks like an alien planet out there, a desolate planet of ice and snow, where they could all die and no one would notice or care. They are alone in this wasteland, abandoned by everything but the faintest glimmer of hope. The cold is no longer a potential threat. It is real, and a part of them now. The diner provides limited shelter, but like everything else it is slowly being consumed by snow and ice. Through the blown-out windows it comes, steadily accumulating across the furniture and floor, across them. Now and then one of them shakes off the flakes the way one might swat away a bug, but it does little good, they're simply going through the motions while trying to ignore the inevitable. The storm is slowly devouring them. And all the while, somewhere out there The Dealer skulks about in the darkness, waiting for them to die.

If they remain here he won't have long to wait.

And yet this night feels different somehow from all the rest. *She* feels different, as if she's experienced some sort of awakening. Despite the mayhem and horror, there is something more here. Something divine. Something that makes her realize there are deeper forces at work on this stormy night.

Greer wipes snow from her eyes and shivers. Luke's death replays in her mind on an endless loop, and though she tries her best to dismiss it, the harder she attempts to ignore it the more vivid it becomes, as if her own mind has turned on her, or as if it's been infiltrated by something beyond her ability to resist.

Like some sick game, she thinks.

Huddled on the floor, shoulder-to-shoulder with Doc and Kit, she subtly takes them in. Kit sits staring straight ahead, eyes wide behind her eyeglass lenses, knees drawn up to her chest, arms wrapped around her calves, chin resting on the tops of her knees. Her lips move but she makes no sound. At first Greer mistakes this for prayer, but then realizes it's merely something similar. She's doing her best to remember and convince herself of what, in her mind, is real and what is not. There is something about the young woman that doesn't sit right with Greer, but she can't quite put her finger on it. Years in sales have taught her how to effectively read people, and something with Kit seems off, as if she knows or suspects something she hasn't yet revealed. It's subtle but it's there. But then, fear does strange things to people, so who can be sure?

Doc, on the other hand, is laser-focused on the storm, mumbling incoherent spells and incantations only he seems to grasp.

As Greer returns her attentions to the night, an odd feeling comes over her, something akin to calm. She can only hope it is not acceptance. They have to fight. If they don't they'll surely die. Even if they do, odds are they won't survive the night, so why not go out on their own terms rather than submitting to the storm and allowing that ghoul to come and pick their bones?

Yet she and the others remain on the floor, backs to the lunch counter, watching the front of the diner, the snow blowing in as inside gradually becomes one with outside. They wait, but for what? The inevitable?

"I don't want to die here," Greer says just above a whisper, her breath tumbling from her mouth and nostrils like smoke.

No one answers. *Maybe they didn't hear me*, she thinks. Or maybe there is no answer. Maybe there's nothing left to say.

She thinks back to her office, remembers standing outside her boss's office and gazing out over the sea of cubicles. She remembers the people, soulless drones shuffling through their lives, joyless and broken, and is reminded why she so preferred being on the road.

In particular, Greer remembers an older woman from the accounting department—Brenda her name was—who would always corner her whenever she returned from the road as if she were a glamorous celebrity that had descended upon their otherwise drab and tedious lives. Longingly, she'd ask, "How is it out there?"

Just as empty as it is here.

In her eyes Greer saw the same things she notices in nearly everyone else she encounters, the need to feel something beyond basic existence. People do things to feel alive. Sex, drugs, violence, religion and other vices exist to better help them remember what it feels like to be human. But just like prayer, in some ways these things strand them and save them all at once. *Are these real memories then,* she wonders, *or lies I've been told to believe?*

If the monster out there truly is of the Devil then where is God in all this? Where is His emissary? Is it Doc, with his shotgun, spells, magic potions, superstitions and prayers? Was it Luke, a selectively loyal disciple and sacrificial lamb? Could it be Kit, the one who doesn't believe in any of this and claims to have no idea why fate has led her to this place and time?

Or am I the one?

What if there is no emissary? What if God is far away from this awful place and we're on our own? What if we always are, always have been? What if God abandoned us long ago and something else is in charge of this nightmare, controlling us all like puppets on invisible strings? What if ours is a false god?

"We could hide in one of the rooms," Kit says, her voice barely audible above the gusting wind. "If we can make it to the rooms we—"

"You'd be cornered there with no way out."

"And we're not here?"

"Not if he comes to us."

Kit looks to Greer. "What do you think?"

"I'm freezing," Greer answers. "We can't stay here like this, we'll die."

"He'll come," Doc says.

"And then?"

"Then you two make your run for it. Because then it's just him and me."

Kit reaches over and clutches Greer's forearm. "I say we try to make it to the rooms now. If he wants to stay here, fine."

"You won't make it," Doc tells them. "And even if by some miracle you do, how will you keep him out? The only chance you have is if he's focused on something else. Once he comes to us, he will be. He'll be focused on me."

"What if we can't wait that long?"

"If you go now you won't make it."

"If we stay here we won't either. What's the difference?"

"She's right," Greer agrees. "If we try to wait him out we'll freeze to death. We'll have no chance. If we try to make it to a room now we may have a slim chance, but it's better than no chance at all."

"You have no idea what you're dealing with."

"Look," Kit says, scrambling onto her knees, "I know you've been through hell with this man, and you've said and done a lot of things tonight, many of them quite compelling, but I've seen nothing that indicates we're dealing with anything other than a human being. Granted, a sick and highly dangerous human being that'll stop at nothing to kill us, but a human being nonetheless."

"God—"

"There is no God. Not here."

Doc sighs. "No. There isn't. Is there."

"If the snow gets much deeper out there," Kit reminds him, "we won't be able to get out of here, much less across the property to the units. We have to make the move *now*."

He looks to Greer.

"She's right, Doc."

"Then we have to do something to draw him to us."

"Like what?" Kit asks.

"Like bait."

"What do you want me to do?"

"Not you. Me." Doc gets to his knees. "While he's been hunting others, I've been hunting him. So if I go to him it won't seem strange. In fact, he might even be expecting it. He's waiting us out but sooner or later if I don't go for him, he'll come for us. So I'll go for him now, and I mean straight for him."

"But you don't know where he is," Greer says.

"He dragged Luke's body around the side of the office, so I'll head that way. The minute he shows and I have his attention, you two make a break for it."

"OK," Greer says. "And then what?"

"You hunker down and hope for the best. If he doesn't take me down out there, I'll lure him back here, and once he's here, well...then it's just the two of us, and it's my fight."

Something changes in the night and catches Kit's eye. She looks out at the storm. Light...dancing and moving through the darkness, bleeding through the walls of snow...orange flickering light accompanied by an odd rumbling sound barely audible above the wind...

"Jesus," she mumbles.

Along with the others, she scurries to the front wall and peers through the blown-out windows.

The motel, from office to the last unit, is on fire.

NINETEEN

"He's burning it down," Greer mumbles. "He's burning it all down. There's nowhere left to go, we—"

"The shed," Kit says. "The storage shed. There's no heat but we can close it up tight and at least get shelter from the storm."

Doc turns from the windows and starts for the back. "Change of plans." He disappears into the kitchen then returns a moment later, grabs something from his bag and sidles up next to Greer. "I'm going to get out there and try to bring him to us. Once I've got him, you and Kit head out the back."

"Once you've *got* him?"

"You'll understand when it happens. There's a pair of gas tanks at the rear of the kitchen. Just checked them, they're a little under half full." He takes Greer's hand and thrusts an object into her palm. Until her fingers curl around it and she holds it up closer for a better look, she doesn't realize it's a grenade. "On your way out, pull the pin and toss that under the tanks. You'll have fifteen seconds before it detonates, so make sure that door is already open when you make the throw. Then run like hell."

"We can't just leave you behind."

"You're not leaving me behind. You're saving yourselves while I stop this sack of shit once and for all." Doc forces a sad smile. "From the moment this started tonight, I've never had any illusions of leaving here alive." He looks to the windows. "We've got to move. You two get into position and sit tight. If I don't come back..." Doc reaches into his jacket, pulls free the crystal and holds it out for Kit. "This'll be your only shot."

"But I don't know how to use it," Kit tells him.

"You will."

"How? I—"

"Kit." He pushes it into her hand and gives it a squeeze. "You'll *know*."

"I don't hear the music, Doc. No angelic choirs or chants."

"Maybe I don't either."

"Yes, you do."

"You sure about that?"

She nods. "I want to hear them too, believe me I do. I just don't think I can."

His bloodshot eyes find hers in the dark. "You'd be surprised."

Kit looks away, unsure of what to do or say.

"Just remember," he tells them, "either way, the flesh can't just die, it has to be annihilated. The host is doomed. The flesh dies and the parasite's bound."

Greer reaches out, touches Doc's shoulder. Though she says nothing more and neither does he, many things pass between them in those few cold and quiet moments. And then, shotgun in hand, Doc topples the furniture from the doorway, crouches, then heads out, disappearing into the storm.

The snow is to his knees. Doc pushes his way a few feet from the diner but it's extremely slow going, and with the constant whirl of flakes, he can only see a foot or so ahead of him at most. He stops, exhausted after less than twenty yards, and drops down, hoping the visibility might be greater the closer to the ground he gets.

The motel burns steadily, crackling and raging as the fire spreads from one unit to the next. The office is completely engulfed in flames. The heat hits him in waves, a bizarre feeling in the middle of a blizzard, but there it is. Despite the wind, the temperature is up all across the property, but he knows the fire can only last so long in such conditions, and soon the cold will again take control as ice and snow locks everything down and buries them all.

Doc scans the area between his position and the motel. He can see nothing but night and snowflakes. But he feels The Dealer. He's close.

Here kitty-kitty.

He looks behind him. He's not far from the diner but it's barely visible, a dark silhouette in the snowy night. He turns back toward the motel, scans the area again as best he can.

Come on, you sonofabitch.

Swinging his hips, he throws one leg forward then the other, shifting his way through the snow as a gust of wind slams him, reminding that the heat from the fires offer nothing more than false and transient hope. Doc comes to a stop, out of breath and blinded by snow. He wipes ice from his face with the back of his hand. He can't risk going much farther or he'll never make it back to the diner. The heat hits him again and he allows himself a moment to embrace it.

A shadowy form suddenly springs up through the snow in front of him in a spray of powder. The Dealer, arms extended and lunging for him, head and face covered with Luke's ski mask.

Doc fires but the barrel is at too high of an angle and goes off over The Dealer's shoulder. While the blast alone should've deafened him, The Dealer is unfazed. The wide and crazed whites of his eyes burn through the snow and darkness as his hands find Doc's throat and clamp down with remarkable power.

Doc swings the shotgun up, slams the butt up under The Dealer's chin. The blow snaps his head back and his grip softens but doesn't release. Bringing the shotgun back around, he strikes him with the butt again, this time full in the mouth. It breaks the grip on Doc's throat and The Dealer staggers back in the snow, blood and teeth flying about with the snowflakes.

Doc racks the shotgun, but The Dealer is already on him, punching a hand into his midsection that lands with such force it knocks Doc off his feet and back into the deep snow. But it isn't until Doc rolls over, frantically kicking his legs and swinging his arms as if to swim through the snow and back to his feet, that he realizes something is wrong. Terribly wrong.

A burning sensation in his stomach fans out into his sides and up across his chest, quickly morphing into a sharp and agonizing pain that explodes through his entire body like a sunburst.

Back to his feet, he seems unable to draw a full breath. The Dealer has vanished. Doc is alone in the storm. He staggers, realizes he's dropped the shotgun at some point. He also realizes his hands are wet, though not with snow and ice. His midsection is soaked. *Blood, I—I'm bleeding, he—Christ, the fucker stabbed me.*

Bent forward at the waist, blood and vomit spray from his mouth as he frantically searches for the shotgun. He quickly finds the barrel protruding from the snow to his right, and battling through what has become excruciating pain, takes it up and heads back toward the diner.

Doc falls face-first into the snow after only a few shuffling steps. He can barely breathe, and he is becoming lightheaded. The wound is bad, and he knows it, but he cannot give in to the pain and fear. Not now.

He pushes on through the heavy snow, hopeful The Dealer is following, toying with him the way a cat allows a mouse to get nearly to the end of its reach before snatching it back for the kill.

Once the diner is within reach he pushes through the snow and falls against the blown-out doorway. Freezing and racked with pain, Doc stumbles into the diner, dragging the shotgun along with him. He cannot see Kit or Greer but knows they're there, hiding in the shadows near the door to the kitchen and waiting for his signal.

He spins back toward the door.

There, at the threshold, is The Dealer. Standing mere feet away, a large knife in hand, the blade soaked and dripping with Doc's blood. The ski mask still covers his face, but the yellow eyes have returned, peering at him from the holes in the mask. The opening for the mouth is slick with blood.

So many years, Doc thinks. *I've dreamed about this moment.*

He steps back, tries to raise the shotgun but apparently can't. Instead his legs give out and he falls onto the seat of his pants over by the lunch counter. The shotgun is still clutched in one hand, but he can't seem to lift it, as if he no longer has the strength.

He appears helpless, and The Dealer knows it.

The Dealer peels the ski mask off and tosses it away over his shoulder. His mouth is a bloody mess. Chest heaving, he watches the darkness of the diner awhile and Doc awhile longer still, saying nothing, doing nothing. Just watching.

It looks like a man. Moves like a man. Bleeds like a man. But this is no man.

"You know who I am," Doc says, blood slurring his speech. "You remember me. You remember my family. My wife... my little girl..."

He finally takes a step into the diner. "I remember how warm their blood felt on my skin," he growls. "And I remember they died screaming and calling for *you*. Right until the end, they thought you'd save them."

You're mine, you fuck, and you don't even know it.

"This ends now."

The Dealer smiles with his bloody gums and broken teeth.

"Bring it, motherfucker," Doc says. "Come on."

As he starts toward him, knife raised, Doc suddenly raises the shotgun with both hands and fires.

The impact of the blast throws The Dealer against the wall as his abdomen is blown apart. His face twisted into a confused grimace, he topples over lifelessly and slumps into a sitting position, a wide red wake smearing the wall behind him.

Doc, no longer able to hold the shotgun up, lets it drop down into his lap.

"Doc!" Greer calls from the darkness behind him.

"Stay there," he gasps, "don't—this isn't over."

Impossibly, The Dealer raises his head, coughs, spits blood and slowly begins struggling to his feet. Still clutching the knife, he stumbles forward, blood and viscera dripping and dangling from his destroyed abdomen.

It isn't until he is within a foot or two of Doc that he stops and looks back then all around, like someone suddenly under attack by a swarm of bees. He stumbles again and his expression reveals the level of his confusion.

Doc coughs. Blood pours from his mouth and he gags, but he too struggles to his feet.

The wind blows hard, displacing some snow on the floor, enough so that the traces of linoleum beneath become visible.

Along with the markings in chalk Doc made there earlier.

The Dealer's eyes grow wide and wild. "No," he says, whispered at first. And then, louder and more panicked. "NO!"

He begins flailing about in an attempt to get back out the doorway, but he appears to be blocked by some invisible barricade.

Greer and Kit step far enough from the shadows to see the circle Doc drew on the floor, a circle with a pentagram in the center that has trapped The Dealer within it.

"No!" he screams again. He tries desperately to step out of the circle again and again but is unable to do so.

"Doc!" Greer screams, running toward him. "You're hurt, you—"

"Stay back!" Doc says, winching in pain.

Greer stops, hands to her mouth.

Back on his feet, Doc reaches a hand out to Kit. "The crystal."

Kit stares at him as if in a trance.

"Kit, goddamn it, the circle won't hold forever! The crystal!"

She throws it to him.

He catches it and staggers into the circle with The Dealer.

Blood and bodily fluids spill onto the floor, spattering across the circle, but both men remain standing and facing each other, The Dealer still clutching his knife and Doc holding tight to the crystal, allowing it to dangle and swing free on its satin cord so his adversary is sure to see it.

The Dealer does, and, struggling for breath, wildly shakes his head. "You can't stop me. I'm going to wear your skin while you still breathe."

"Better hurry."

"I'm a god! I—I'm going home! I'm going home!"

Doc reaches for him, but The Dealer is ready, and again slams the knife into him. Greer and Kit run to the very edge of the circle but stop just outside it as The Dealer yanks the blade free and stabs Doc again.

He groans, gags and drops to his knees, but he brings The Dealer with him and together they fall to their knees in the center of the circle. As Doc struggles to remain conscious and upright, The Dealer rears back with the knife for a third strike.

Before he can complete the thrust, Greer pulls the commando knife free from her belt, steps into the circle and with a scream of rage and horror, slams the blade into the side of The Dealer's neck.

It impales him, easily stabbing straight through his throat and trapping the blade in his neck. Greer lets go and scrambles away as Doc grabs the handle and pulls it free. Ribbons of blood spurt from The Dealer's neck as the knife falls to the floor. His eyes roll to white then back, as the bloodbath continues, flowing from both men now into the circle and filling it with crimson.

Doc wraps one arm around The Dealer's head, pulling him close so that their blood cheeks touch. Gurgling and choking on his own blood, The Dealer attempts to pull away, but Doc holds him with every ounce of strength he has left.

"In the name of God," he slurs, "I bind this evil."

"No," The Dealer struggles to get free, but Doc presses the crystal to his cheek, which seems to help hold him in place. "You can't do this you—"

"I bind you, demon, and all your evil works and powers." Doc chokes, coughs out more blood and nearly falls. No longer strong enough to hold onto The Dealer, he lets go, but the spell has begun, and The Dealer remains where he is, thrashing about like a madman, his body jerking about and moving at impossible speeds. "I order you to go where I send you. I bind you and command you to stay there, in the name of God. You... unclean, foul and demonic spirit, are bound forever, for eternity."

The Dealer becomes still, but for a slow swaying to his upper body. His yellow eyes burn no more, and he remains on his knees, decidedly human eyes transfixed on the crystal now, as it dangles before him.

"Amen," Doc gasps.

The Dealer falls forward into Doc's arms. He wraps his arms around him and they both fall back atop each other. As he lands, his hand falls back and out of the circle, the crystal just barely still in his grasp. Eyes slowly dying, he finds Greer and nods.

Tears streaming her face, she nods back, turns and runs for the back.

A moment later Kit follows.

As Doc lies dying in the dark and cold, entangled with the dead body atop him, he closes his eyes, tries to ignore the pain and blood filling his lungs and thinks instead of Karen and Jodi. Of all that was lost, and all he hopes he will find again beyond this darkness, where light dwells and where all that has been lost will again be found.

I'm going home.

TWENTY

By the time Kit reaches the backroom, Greer already has the door open and is holding it against the wind as snow blows into the stockroom in heavy icy gusts. "Hurry!"

Knapsack held tight to her chest, Kit holds the door with her shoulder and gives a decisive nod.

As demonic growls and cries that sound somewhere between agonizing pain and unimaginable rage echo through the darkness in the diner, Greer pulls the pin and rolls the grenade under the gas tanks. "Go!"

Kit bolts into the storm, Greer right behind her.

Freezing wind burns their flesh and lungs and makes their eyes tear, while the deep snow makes their legs feel like they've been submerged in wet cement up to their thighs. But they keep running as best they can, shuffling forward and forcing their way through the storm.

One explosion is quickly followed by a second.

Incredible force slams into them from behind, sending them sprawling and cartwheeling through the night.

Greer flies through the darkness, across an embankment and into a thick drift of snow. The last thing she sees is Kit tumbling away into curtains of night and snow like a piece of debris riding the wind.

The house is an old Victorian Greer doesn't recognize. Everything in it is dated and old. Everything is black-and-white and Greer feels like everything—including herself—is moving in slow motion. Almost as if she's just emerged from a deep sleep but hasn't yet fully escaped it, isn't yet completely conscious. But doesn't she dream in color? She thinks she does. In fact, she's sure of it.

So this must not be a dream then. This must be something...else.

She moves through the foyer and sees a large and winding ornate staircase that leads to the second floor. Everything here is dark and yet the windows reveal it is daytime. But even the light is different here, muted and strange. She looks around at the old furniture and worn paintings hanging in bulky wooden frames, enormous formal portraits hanging on the walls and scattered throughout the house.

They're all there, all of them represented.

Doc... Luke... Carlin... Greer herself...

She moves closer to her own portrait, gazes up at it. She has no memory of ever having sat for such a painting. A shiver rattles her to the bone, and she hugs herself. It's freezing in here. Doesn't the house have heat?

Greer looks at her hands. They are cold, raw, red and sore.

She doesn't want to be here but understands somehow that she must be. It is not a choice.

Greer slowly climbs the stairs, following the long staircase up to the landing on the second floor. A narrow hallway with doors on either side runs the length of the house in both directions. She can go left or right, but chooses left, because at the far end of that section of hallway, a lone door stands open.

She follows the hallway, feels the old floorboards creak and moan with each step, and finally reaches the open doorway.

Inside, but for a small table and chair in the center, the room is completely empty and painted entirely in white. In the center of the table sits an old and worn deck of playing cards, neatly stacked.

Kit stands before a long, tall window, the only one in the room. Because there are no curtains, inordinately bright shafts of daylight cascade through the room and along the walls and floor, eerie in the otherwise drab house.

"Kit?"

She glances back over her shoulder, stone-faced, but says nothing. One of her eyeglass lenses sports a web-like crack. She seems not to notice.

Greer slowly crosses the room and joins her at the window.

Outside, the yard below is dead and gray. There is no snow, but the world is sheathed in ice, even the dead trees lining the edge of the property and towering over the house like forgotten and crippled sentries have not been spared.

She cannot clearly see past the wall of trees, but it appears as if a solid, beveled, and intricately formed wall of ice stands just beyond them.

It's like some sort of prison, Greer thinks, a glacial prison of ice and cold.

"Kit... where are we?"

Everything is impossibly still outside. No wind. No motion. No life.

"Are we dead?" Greer asks, her voice weak and tired.

Kit slowly turns her head and looks at her. "Not yet."

Behind them, out in the hallway, the floor creaks. Someone... something is coming...

"There's something here," Greer says, "in the house with us."

"Yes. There is."

Greer clenches shut her eyes as fear rises, slithering through her like a serpent coiling around her spine. Despite the cold, all she sees in the darkness of her mind are flames. "Am I dreaming?"

"No," Kit whispers. "I am."

TWENTY-ONE

lthough it's only late afternoon, it's already getting dark. A gentle though ominous rain falls over the city as a woman in a trench coat, dark dress and heels hurries through the shadows of a narrow alley, finally ducking under an awning over the stoop at the rear of a Chinese restaurant. A small Asian man in a bloody apron sits on an overturned crate smoking a cigarette, obvious to the weather. He glances at the woman with disinterest then looks away, back down the alley, as if expecting someone or something else to follow her.

The woman, mid-thirties, dark-haired, pretty and petite, escapes through the door, crosses through a busy kitchen and the unwelcome stares of several cooks and workers and pushes through a swinging door into a small, candlelit but otherwise dark dining area. She hesitates a moment, eyes scanning the room. Three Asian waiters stand against the kitchen wall in a formal row.

There are no booths here, only tables outfitted with dark red tablecloths and small single candles in squat red globes.

It all feels like a dream, but it's real. She wishes it wasn't, but knows it is.

All but two of the tables are unoccupied. A young couple sits at one while a dwarf of perhaps fifty sits at the other.

With a purposeful stride the woman walks to a table in back. Cloaked in shadow and candlelight, the dwarf sits alone at the table, a lighter and pack of cigarettes before him, along with an exotic-looking drink complete with paper umbrella. Dressed in an ill-fitting suit, he straightens his tie even though it doesn't need straightening, clears his throat and looks up at the woman with an expressionless, decidedly reptilian-like gaze.

From hidden speakers Ella Fitzgerald quietly sings *The Nearness of You.*

"I'm in trouble," she tells him.

He selects a cigarette from the pack and rolls it into the corner of his mouth. "I've always had a soft spot for women in peril." After lighting the cigarette he motions to the chair across from him.

She removes her raincoat, puts it over the back of the chair and joins him, nervously looking back over her shoulder before continuing the conversation. "We've made a terrible mistake."

The dwarf exhales through his nose, eyes slowly blinking.

"They thought it didn't work," she says desperately. "But it did."

"It was a failure."

"No. It wasn't."

"The entire thing was scrapped years ago."

"They didn't wait long enough." The woman brings a trembling hand to her face. "Things are... *happening*."

He sips his drink. "Drink? Something to eat? The duck here is positively orgasmic."

She shakes her head no.

The dwarf holds a hand up, stopping an approaching waiter before he reaches the table, then returns his attention to the woman. He draws on his cigarette, staring at her through the spirals of smoke. "You were told side-effects were always a possibility."

"You don't understand. I'm telling you it worked. Maybe not at first, maybe not even for years, but—"

"The program no longer exists. In fact, it never did."

"But—"

"Even if after all this time I could contact the proper channels and let them know there's been a new development that requires their attention, which is highly doubtful, you must realize their solution will be immediate quarantine and probable termination. Then again, if what you're saying is true, that may not only be best, it may be wholly necessary." He butts his cigarette in a glass ashtray on the table. "We can't always wait for nature to thin the herd, now can we?"

"Interesting philosophy," she says, "especially coming from you."

He takes another sip of his drink. "You really should have one of these. It's called a Volcano. No idea what's in it but it's delicious. Rum, I think."

"I'm afraid of my own child." The woman's eyes turn moist. "She's only a teenager and I'm terrified of her. I love her, but her imagination frightens me. In a few years she'll be capable of things no one will be able to stop."

"As e.e. cummings wrote… *'To destroy is always the first step in any creation,'*" he says. "Meaning if by some slim chance you're right, then it's wise to be afraid."

"If I am… it would make her—*God*—wouldn't it?"

The dwarf licks his lips, remembering her nude pregnant body on display all those years ago. "Don't be silly." He reaches across the table and gently pats her hand with his tiny fingers. "There is no God."

TWENTY-TWO

Something tickles open her heavy eyelids. As the world slowly blends into dark focus, Greer realizes she's lying on her back watching an endless mass of snowflakes descending upon her. For what seems an eternity she cannot move, or perhaps doesn't really try to. She just lays there, cold and dazed and unsure of what's happening. But the memories slowly return and the jumble of disjointed and frenzied thoughts firing through her head eventually becomes more coherent and she realizes where she is.

She tries to move her arms and legs and finds that although they're stiff and sore, she is able to do so. She rolls over and into a sitting position.

Falling over against a large drift of packed snow, Greer sees the piles of rubble that were once the motel and diner. They are still burning, the debris crackling and popping, shooting occasional showers of sparks high into the air. Even at a considerable distance the heat from the flames flush her face.

A faint cough slips through the wind-sounds.

Greer wipes snow from her eyes with a trembling hand.

The illumination from the flames cast shadows across the snow, revealing someone a few feet away: Kit, on hands and knees.

At first both are too shaken and exhausted to speak, but Kit sees her and eventually crawls closer.

"Is it over?" Greer asks breathlessly.

Kit falls against the drift a few feet from her, mouth open and eyeglasses cracked. She nods. Or maybe she only shivers. Neither can be sure. "Are you all right?" Kit asks.

"I'm alive... I think."

"For now. The fire's helping but it won't burn long in this storm. Once it's out we're done."

"The fire, the explosions... someone had to see it."

"Maybe."

"You think they'll find us out here?"

"Not sure they could get to us right now even if they wanted to."

"They wouldn't just leave us out here, would they?"

"Even if they do get to us, might not be in time."

Both have seen that the explosions also toppled the shed they had planned to use for shelter, but neither mentions it. There seems little point.

"Why did everything have to be destroyed like this?"

"Doc said the flesh of the host had to be annihilated. We had no choice."

"It stopped The Dealer, but it doomed us too."

"Maybe we were already doomed."

Greer wipes her nose. She thinks it's running until her hand comes back slick with blood. Normally a nosebleed would upset her, but what difference does it make now?

Kit reaches into her jacket and hands her a crumpled tissue.

Greer takes it, holds it under her nose a moment then tosses it aside.

After a moment, Kit shows her what's in her other hand, the crystal, dangling from its satin cord, swaying in the wind and sparkling in the snow and firelight.

"You took it?"

"Doc was holding it, but his hand was outside the circle. He wanted me to."

"It should've gone up in flames with them."

"I was supposed to take it, that's what Doc wanted."

Greer lets it go. "So now what?"

"It needs to be hidden somewhere no one's ever going to find it."

"How are you going to do that?"

"I don't know."

"If we bury it in the snow, when it eventually melts, someone will find it."

Kit removes her glasses and paws ice from her eyes with a shaking hand. "Sometimes the best place to hide is in plain sight. If I don't make it they'll find me out here, but they won't know what this is." She reaches out into the snow, retrieves her knapsack and drags it closer. "They'll think it's just cheap jewelry."

Greer stares at her awhile. "I don't think I can feel my feet."

"Me either."

"Aren't you afraid?"

"Of what?"

Greer motions to the crystal.

"Doc said he was trapped for eternity unless someone lets him out."

"Thought you didn't believe in any of that."

Kit shivers. "Do you still hear him talking to you?"

Greer shakes her head no.

"You sure?"

"Yes I'm sure. Don't you trust me?"

"Do you trust me?"

"Should I?"

The wind howls, blowing snow about between them.

"You think he got to me?" Greer asks evenly. "You think he wore me down, confused me and tricked his way into me at the last minute?"

Kit watches her closely but offers no response.

"Maybe you're the one," Greer says. "You've got the crystal."

"I wish I could hear what Doc heard."

"The angels..."

"Yeah," she says as clouds of breath dance around her. "Even if it's not real, I still wish I could hear it. Just once."

Greer notices the knapsack. "Managed to save that, huh?"

"It's got my novel in it. My laptop was destroyed so this is the only copy I have left."

Greer adjusts her position a bit, but it's becoming harder and harder to move. "What's it about anyway?"

"A small group of people trapped at a roadside motel in the middle of a blizzard being terrorized by a demonic killer."

Greer smiles through the pain and cold. "Sounds scary."

"It is."

"How's it end?"

"I don't know. I never got a chance to finish it."

"Maybe it doesn't have an end."

"Everything has an end."

A heavy gust of wind blows, and along with the endless parade of snowflakes… playing cards… an entire deck… flutter through the air and rain down from the dark sky all around them, littering the snow with hearts and spades, clubs and diamonds and the bloody ghosts of those who came before them.

It is then that Greer realizes she's not joking. Wearily, she reaches for the knife on her belt then remembers it's no longer there. "I don't think we're going to make it."

"Then it doesn't really matter, does it?"

"No, I guess not."

"Maybe it's best this way."

"Maybe so."

The cold is becoming painful, and her body is shutting down. Greer can feel it gradually turning off, like she's fading away into oblivion, becoming one with the storm. She knows she shouldn't close her eyes but can't seem to prevent it from happening. Her mind blurs… slows…

Kit stuffs the crystal into the knapsack, holds it tight against her chest and gazes at the cards in the snow. "Up for some midnight solitaire?"

"Solitaire's played alone."

"I am alone."

"A writer spinning tales. Like God."

"You think God's a writer?"

"I think God's alone. Like all gods, He's hopelessly, desperately alone. Even when He's not."

"Or even when *she's* not."

"Yes," Greer agrees. "Even when *she's* not."

Kit leans her head back in the snow and thinks of her mother, how she will never see her again and how these kinds of things have always terrified her so. Yes, maybe it really is best this way. "But I don't believe in God," she says. "Remember?"

"Maybe that's because you *are* God."

With what little strength she has left, Kit begins to laugh.

But in the swirling howl of blizzard winds, there is no one there to hear it.

THE END?

Not if you want to dive into more of Crystal Lake Publishing's Tales from the Darkest Depths!

Check out our amazing website and online store or download our latest catalog here: https://geni.us/CLPCatalog

We always have great new projects and content on the website to dive into, as well as a newsletter, behind the scenes options, social media platforms, our own dark fiction shared-world series and our very own webstore. Our webstore even has categories specifically for KU books, non-fiction, anthologies, and of course more novels and novellas.

AUTHOR BIOGRAPHY

Described as 'The best writer of horror and thrillers at work today' by author Christopher Rice, and praised as one of the best writers of his generation by authors including Ed Gorman, Brian Keene and the legendary author of Six Days of the Condor, James Grady, among others, Greg F. Gifune is a best-selling, internationally-published author of several acclaimed novels, novellas, screenplays, and two short story collections. Working predominantly in the horror and crime genres, Gifune's work has been translated into several languages, has received starred reviews from Publisher's Weekly, Library Journal and others, and is consistently praised by readers and critics alike. His novel THE BLEEDING SEASON, originally published in 2003, has been hailed as a classic in the horror/suspense genres, and is considered by many, including *Famous Monsters of Filmland*, to be one of the best horror novels of its kind ever written. Gifune is also working on several film projects as both a writer and producer, consults on film and TV scripts, and helps punch-up projects for other authors, screenwriters and filmmakers. For film/TV he is represented by Paradigm Talent Agency in Hollywood. Greg resides in Massachusetts with his wife and their dogs, and can be reached online at gfgauthor@verizon.net or on Facebook, Twitter and Instagram.

Readers…

Thank you for reading *Midnight Solitaire*. We hope you enjoyed this novel.

Help other readers by telling them why you enjoyed this book. No need to write an in-depth discussion. Even a single sentence will be greatly appreciated. Reviews go a long way to helping a book sell, and is great for an author's career. It'll also help us to continue publishing quality books.

Thank you again for taking the time to journey with Crystal Lake Publishing.

You will find links to all our social media platforms on our Linktree page:
https://linktr.ee/CrystalLakePublishing.

MISSION STATEMENT

Since its founding in August 2012, Crystal Lake Publishing has quickly become one of the world's leading publishers of Dark Fiction and Horror books in print, eBook, and audio formats.

While we strive to present only the highest quality fiction and entertainment, we also endeavour to support authors along their writing journey. We offer our time and experience in non-fiction projects, as well as author mentoring and services, at competitive prices.

With several Bram Stoker Award wins and many other wins and nominations (including the HWA's Specialty Press Award), Crystal Lake Publishing puts integrity, honor, and respect at the forefront of our publishing operations.

We strive for each book and outreach program we spearhead to not only entertain and touch or comment on issues that affect our readers, but also to strengthen and support the Dark Fiction field and its authors.

Not only do we find and publish authors we believe are destined for greatness, but we strive to work with men and woman who endeavour to be decent human beings who care more for others than themselves, while still being hard working, driven, and passionate artists and storytellers.

Crystal Lake Publishing is and will always be a beacon of what passion and dedication, combined with overwhelming teamwork and respect, can accomplish. We endeavour to know each and every one of our readers, while building personal relationships with our authors, reviewers, bloggers, podcasters, bookstores, and libraries.

We will be as trustworthy, forthright, and transparent as any business can be, while also keeping most of the headaches away from our authors, since it's our job to solve the problems so they can stay in a creative mind. Which of course also means paying our authors.

We do not just publish books, we present to you worlds within your world, doors within your mind, from talented authors who sacrifice so much for a moment of your time.

There are some amazing small presses out there, and through collaboration and open forums we will continue to support other presses in the goal of helping authors and showing the world what quality small presses are capable of accomplishing. No one wins when a small press goes down, so we will always be there to support hardworking, legitimate presses and their authors. We don't see Crystal Lake as the best press out there, but we will always strive to be the best, strive to be the most interactive and grateful, and even blessed press around. No matter what happens over time, we will also take our mission very seriously while appreciating where we are and enjoying the journey.

What do we offer our authors that they can't do for themselves through self-publishing?

We are big supporters of self-publishing (especially hybrid publishing), if done with care, patience, and planning. However, not every author has the time or inclination to do market research, advertise, and set up book launch strategies. Although a lot of authors are successful in doing it all, strong small presses will always be there for the authors who just want to do what they do best: write.

What we offer is experience, industry knowledge, contacts and trust built up over years. And due to our strong brand and trusting fanbase, every Crystal Lake Publishing book comes with weight of respect. In time our fans begin to trust our judgment and will try a new author purely based on our support of said author.

With each launch we strive to fine-tune our approach, learn from our mistakes, and increase our reach. We continue to assure our authors that we're here for them and that we'll carry the weight of the launch and dealing with third parties while they focus on their strengths—be it writing, interviews, blogs, signings, etc.

We also offer several mentoring packages to authors that include knowledge and skills they can use in both traditional and self-publishing endeavours.

We look forward to launching many new careers.

This is what we believe in. What we stand for. This will be our legacy.

Welcome to Crystal Lake Publishing—Tales from the Darkest Depths.

THANK YOU FOR PURCHASING THIS BOOK

www.ingramcontent.com/pod-product-compliance
Lightning Source LLC
Chambersburg PA
CBHW070512200726

48293CB00007B/2497